T0159149

WHEN THE LANES COME TOGETHER

Chad E Linden

authorHOUSE®

AuthorHouse™
1663 Liberty Drive
Bloomington, IN 47403
www.authorhouse.com
Phone: 1 (800) 839-8640

© *2018 Chad E Linden. All rights reserved.*

No part of this book may be reproduced, stored in a retrieval system, or transmitted by any means without the written permission of the author.

Published by AuthorHouse 11/30/2018

ISBN: 978-1-5462-3492-0 (sc)
ISBN: 978-1-5462-3491-3 (e)

Print information available on the last page.

Any people depicted in stock imagery provided by Getty Images are models, and such images are being used for illustrative purposes only. Certain stock imagery © Getty Images.

This book is printed on acid-free paper.

Because of the dynamic nature of the Internet, any web addresses or links contained in this book may have changed since publication and may no longer be valid. The views expressed in this work are solely those of the author and do not necessarily reflect the views of the publisher, and the publisher hereby disclaims any responsibility for them.

This Book Is Dedicated to memory of George David Lane and Doris Kathleen Lane.

The life my Grandmother lived along with the memories of my Grandfather that she passed on is what made this book what is.

I would also like to give tribute to my Uncle, Donald Allen Lane. He was only a part of a brief portion of my life but he left impressions that are still here today.

The names of characters I have created were all taken directly from their family tree. I also have used several birthdays and anniversaries that some of my family members might recognize.

The story I have created was built from the memories I have as a child. Some the names and landmarks actually do exist but both are used as fiction in this book. My goal throughout this entire book is to honor not only the people I have mentioned. I want to also honor all those who knew them as well.

DON LANE

The alarm was set for six thirty. By the time the buzzer went off Don was usually up putting on his tennis shoes and getting ready for his morning jog. Many things had changed over the years, but this part of his life had always been the same. His lifestyle allowed him to set his own hours, but to Don, sleeping in always seemed like wasting part of his day.

The small town he lived in did not seem to wake up till later in the day. Don used the time to jog, work on equipment, and have breakfast.

Ever since his parents and brother moved away making a full breakfast seemed almost a waste of time. A cup of coffee would usually do and sometimes perhaps a bowl of grits. The instant mix he used was a far cry from the home-cooked meals he had as a kid. But living alone, it seemed to be the best way to go.

As Don sat at the table, coffee mug in one hand and the newspaper in the other, his bowl of grits had already been pushed aside. Only bits of the shredded cheese were left behind to linger in the bowl. The *Lubbock Journal* was not as thick as he would like it to be, but it always had a comic section. Don had a habit of reading it last. It served to lighten his mood for any possible bad news in the remaining pages.

Charlie Brown missing the football always made him feel better about the rainstorm predicted for the next day. He snickered as he read the day's edition. He thought about his childhood. He would climb on top of the doghouse, like Snoopy, with his hat, scarf, and goggles, pretending to fly a plane. He was always able to convince his little brother to stand behind him and flap the tails of his scarf to signify the wind while he was in the air. Most of the newspaper was taken to his shop for soaking up grease. The comics, however, were always saved. The newspaper was not only the source of bad news. Over the years, when he could not find his joy, Charlie Brown, Snoopy, and Linus always seemed to be able to lead the way.

As a cotton farmer and pilot, Don seldom found himself wondering what to do with his time. With that in mind, he ran his hands through his dark-brown hair. He nodded and was out the door.

His airplane was a Cessna 182, with its wheel structure modified for more stability on rough terrain. It was painted blue on the top and sides and had a Texas flag on the bottom. He started as a crop duster, but now he flew passengers most of the time. His mechanical abilities earned him the name Mr. Wrench. He put everything he could into it, and although chronic leg cramps were an irritation at times, they seldom slowed him down. Some days seemed to be a carbon copy of the one before, varying only with the seasons.

In the winter there was a shortage of coffee and warm socks. And in the summer, there was a shortage of sweet tea and sunscreen.

The passenger flight was doing today was to a town

about a hundred and twenty miles away, the Buffalo Springs Resort. It was his most common destination.

As part of its travel package, guests were given a guided tour of the landmarks surrounding the resort as well as a bird's-eye view of the resort itself. Don never really saw himself as the tour guide type, but crop dusting only happened certain times of the year. Buffalo Springs was, however, a year-round resort that paid well. So for a couple hours a week, he got paid for doing his favorite thing, flying the *Texas Blue Jay* (his plane) and meeting some neat folks along the way.Don had no quarrel with living alone, but he often found himself rather upset because the family life he once knew had dissolved, and he was left alone. Many times he chose to exclude himself from the activities around town just to avoid seeing what he could not have. Don did not set out to live on his own. He grew up in this house with his dad, mom, and twin brother. The walls were filled with countless memories. Don and Allen's all-night Monopoly games, *Wheel of Fortune* on television, and Mom's sewing machine running in the background. When Don and Allen wrestled with their dad, Mom shook her pointer finger at them all.

Don learned there was a sense of freedom from living alone. He did not have to wait for the hot-water heater to warm up before taking a shower. Nor was he ever in danger of the country music station being too loud. No one would hear him singing at the top his lungs to the songs he knew, although the habit of singing at the top of his lungs was not limited to the confines of his house. Even as he landed at the airfield, where his passengers awaited their ride, he belted out the words to his favorite Alabama song.

As Don took the luggage from the couple about to board his airplane, he was still humming the tune in his head. He put the luggage in the rear compartment and then returned to the front. He offered his hand to the woman to help her aboard.

"Ma'am."

Don tipped his cowboy hat as her husband followed her in.

As Don began to go over the necessary safety protocols, he saw the couple had already joined hands and turned their attention to each other. It seemed clear to Don that at least for the moment, they were not interested in much besides each other. After making sure they were buckled in, he showed them where the exits were and then left it at that. As he prepared for takeoff, he thought his well-rehearsed speech about the lay of the land would go unheard but decided to give his spill anyway once they were in the air.

Don's speech covered some Lubbock history and was usually between fifteen and twenty minutes long, depending on the questions the passengers had. Today he decided to cut it to five minutes and left it to them to ask questions if they were so inclined. For the beginning of the flight, he could have been alone on the plane, and it would have been louder. After about five minutes, Don was back to singing Alabama's greatest hits to himself.

As he flew over the city center, the couple finally started asking questions about the landmarks they could see. The thing they asked about was a statue they could only see part of.Don asked them if they liked rock 'n' roll and said that was a statue of the legendary Buddy Holly made in 1980 by a guy named Grant Speed.

The couple was silent but interested.

Don then said that in 1959, Buddy was leaving a concert in Iowa, and his plane crashed. He was born and raised here, and his memory lived on.

Don also told them about museum that was built in his honor as well.

They said they were country music lovers, they both were born and raised in Alabama Don cracked a smile and nodded. One of them pulled out a cassette tape cover with a familiar picture of the band he had learned to love as well. After a moment of silence, he said, he was born in Lubbock as well. His dad was a cotton farmer for a good part of his childhood. He have all of Alabama's albums and they could play him some mountain music any day of the week.

Don saw the patch of trees that was the landmark for making his descent to the resort. He lowered his voice, and in a somewhat comical tone and he told the couple to make sure that their seatbacks and tray tables were in the upright and locked position as they prepare to make their descent to the Buffalo Springs Resort. He also said please check the area around your seat for any items that may have shifted during flight. On behalf of the entire crew of Texas Blue Jay, we thank you for flying with us today.

As Don turned his focus to the controls, the smirk on his face became a concentrated stare because of the task at hand. When he reached the resort and stopped the plane, he turned his head to face the couple, and the smirk had returned. A moment later, he was retrieving their bags as they made the way down the steps to the ground.

On the return trip, his mind wandered back to when his brother lived with him and the events that led to Allen's move to Indiana, chasing Doris Shields. October 10, 1970.

Allen and Don took the truck into town for the annual county fair. It was a 1969 Dodge pickup their parents bought them for their eighteenth birthday. Their family's farm was west, just off the main interstate. The fall fest was east a mile and half off the highway. There were hayrides, line dancing with the band, and pumpkin tossing. There was also Allen's favorite, the pie-eating contest.

The winner received not only a free pie (besides the one they had just eaten) but also a Dairy Queen ticket worth two ice cream sundaes. Allen knew that after three years winning, he had a reputation to protect.

Don was not really into stuffing his face just to get a free pie and ice cream. He also already knew the outcome of the contest; he knew his brother's appetite all too well. So he followed the crowd to the other side of the town to see what happening over there.

When he got to where the crowd was gathering. He found that the street had been blocked of and it was also lit up brighter than a Yankees game. Then he saw something that really caught his eye. About fifty feet above in the air he saw a pilot, he was focused on the intense concentration that the person had. Then he saw the plane, it had dark black landing gear, with a bright red body, the wing tips as well as the back ruder were out lined in the black.

Don was in love. When it landed it was almost parallel with the crowd. It went further down the street then turned around and taxied towards the crowd until it stopped, where it had landed before. The pilot swiftly hopped out of his seat threw out a rope ladder and climbed out and descended to the ground, and takes a bow for the now cheering crowd. Don was equally as amazed as the rest of the crowd, but he was not cheering. He was so struck at the display he could not fit into words what or how he felt. He did know one thing he had to find out more about that plane.

Meanwhile

As Allen was collecting His winnings, he looked up from his pie, wiped what is left of the whip cream off his face. It was here that he first saw Doris, his first he thought was he was seeing an angel. The brown hair, sparkling smile and cute dimples convinced him, his mission in life was to find that girl. He wasting no time, he began to sift through the crowd of people in the direction that he saw her go. Lucky for him he did not have to go far. He spotted her watching the band on the next street over. She was facing the band with her foot tapping steady with the beat of the music, clapping her hands and cheering for the couples dancing in the square. Allen could not help but to stare, as her hair swayed back and forward with the music. Now in somewhat of a trance he continued to stare a few moments more. Was this love at first sight? Allen was not quite sure how or what he knew, but he was for sure that he knew something was different about her. He also knew he had to take a chance. What good would it be to believe in something if she did not believe it as well?

The upbeat music continued but Doris's feet began to slow, Allen took this as the opportunity he was waiting for. He walked up to her and offering a cup of water introduced himself and tipped his hat. He then made some small talk about how good the band was then pointed out his windmill that is visible from the town. He then told her they that he farmed mostly cotton but have a bit of hay as well.

Doris's first response to her impression of Allen was hard to keep to herself. She of course as a proper young woman of nineteen had been taught not to show her feelings towards a man. She did however think that's it's best not to be rude, if someone offers you a refreshing cup of water and polite conversation the least she could do is be polite in return. She took the water, thanked Allen and introduced herself. She then told him that she lived in a town called Mexia and was on way to Indiana. Her Dad just learned that he had some land there and he wanted to see what it was like. Doris had always loved the fairs so when she saw this one as they passed through she sweet-talked him into stopping She saw a white smear of whip cream on Allen's cheek and began to stare at it. She then asked him if he had been in a food fight. Allen explained that he had just won a pie eating contest while wiping his cheek with the palm of his hand.

Doris's eyes widen as she realized what he was talking about. She had been in the crowd when the adventure took place and now all she could think of was the group of people dumping their faces in the foil pie pans. From where she was standing it looked as though Allen just took a breath and inhaled that pie. Doris took her hanky out and removed the remaining whip cream.

Allen sat at a table with Doris for a while chatting away about the landscape differences between Lubbock and Mexia. Allen mentioned he had a brother and Doris stated that it was just her and her Dad. It seemed to Allen that there was more to that comment than she was letting on but he was trying not to push too much and scare her away. Doris did not know how she felt. She really did not stop at the fair to find a man, but now that she had met Allen, what was all this going to come to. She usually was not inclined to be so neighborly to a man she barely knew but this time something told her this time it would be O.K.

Allen told her several times it was Ok to call him by his first name. Doris however continued call him Mr. Lane. The thing was she knew there was connection there, but she also thought she should just run. Allen frowned when she told him this until she further explained. Doris did not see the use of trying to figure things out between them. After tonight this would all be over. She will be going on to Indiana and Allen will still be here. While Allen listened he scribbled something on a napkin. When she was done he told her what he had been thinking. To make his point instead of calling her Doris, he addressed her as Ms. Shields. First he told her he felt the same way she did, there was something there between them. However, he disagreed that it had to end that night.

He then gave her the napkin he had been scribbling on. He told her they could go as far as they wanted. On the napkin he had written his address. He then explained that when his parents were newlyweds his Dad had to be gone for months at a time. The letters they wrote to each other kept their spark alive.

Allen glanced at his watch, the time that he had arranged to meet with his brother was soon upon him, it was just about then that He saw Don in the distance. Allen yelled and Don swung his head around at the sound of his voice. When he saw Allen he nodded and, made his way over to the table to join him and Doris. Allen introduced Doris to Don and told him that she was passing through on her way to Indiana. Don tipped his hat and nodded Doris is somewhat struck at how much they look alike. In fact, so much so that it was a little weird. She looked at Allen then Don Then Allen again trying to find something that was different between the two. As she pondered the resemblances, it dawned on her that it was time to meet up with her Dad. After a few more minutes of chatting, Doris finally announce that she had to go. Addressing them both as, Mr. Lane she spoke of her promise to her Dad then she stood and began to walk away toward the motel. She then held up the napkin with his address on it. And reminded Allen of his promise to her. Allen put his hand on his heart and left there as if to secure his promise would be kept, Doris just laughed.

As she started to walk away, Allen caught up with her and gave her the Dairy Queen tickets.

Then told her it was something to remember her by. She smiled then said thank you.

Then she made her way up the street where she had promised to meet her dad. As she left she thought of the

Afternoon with Allen she then thought of the brothers. Then with a sigh of relief she knew that without a doubt she would always be able to tell them apart.

Allen watched Doris until she was out of site. He then watched the empty street for a few moments more. Don stepped up beside him, after watching the interchange between his brother and Doris. He did not say anything at first but put his hand on Allen's shoulder. He them looked in the general direction and nodded his head. Don then asked what they were going to do. Allen said that Doris had promised to write him when she gets it Indian, and they had decided that they would start with letters back and forth and see where it goes from there.

Allen and Doris did write each other for a full year. Allen wrote about his life as a cotton farmer's son, then his love for card games and building card house. He then told he how much he liked board games especially monopoly. He told her that he once tried to be an athlete in school but found that he could not keep up. He also told her all the things that he and Don had done as kids growing up, and how close Don and him had become. He told her about when his Dad became a deputy for the Dallas sheriff and their parents had to move to the city. It was hard on Don and him but it had brought them even closer than they were before.

Doris was as equally open with Allen as he was to her. She started by telling him about her dad's decision to move to Indiana. She then she told him of her love for piano playing. She also told him how much she loved to cook, sew, crochet and needlepoint. She had recently learned as an only child when she turned twenty, the land in Indiana would be hers. She kind of chuckled a little when her Dad joked with her about finding a man to help keep the farm going. She also shared her pain about her mother's death several years earlier and the gap it had left in her life. Despite the fact that Allen always ended each letter with his first name Doris began each letter to him with his last.

Allen sat on the couch in his house chatting with Don. After a year of letters back and forth he was feeling like it was time to take the next step. Don and him had gone to the fair the night before just as they had the same time for the last twelve years. This time however Allen was a little too preoccupied to join in the fun. He found himself looking for Doris in the crowd. Once at the benches where that had sat together the year before and another time on the street where the dancing took place. For the first time in five years he did not win the pie eating contest. For the first time in many years that was the last thing on his mind. As he told Don what he wanted to do he nodded in agreement. Allen's plan was simple. The easiest way for him to know if what he felt with Doris was real was he needed to go see her in Indiana. He just need to know.

If Doris was the one, why would he not want to pursue her further. On the other hand, if their giggles and laughs were all it amounted to, Allen did not think it would be fair to either of them to carry on. Allen had this feeling based on their letters that at least on the surface, the goals they had in life were one in the same. The reality is that Allen's personality has kind of two sides, he has somewhat of a dry humor that made Doris giggle when she read his jokes. However, Allen had a sincere side as well. He shared this side of himself when they met by telling Doris about the letters that his parents wrote to each other. When it came to the letters to Doris he was afraid let this side out. He did not want to risk scaring her away. The content of Allen's letters where a very calculated mix of telling her about him, making her laugh and only lightly seasoned with his sincere side, just to be safe.

Allen was about to compose a letter that would do one of two things. He could either create a channel for their hearts to flow together or they could learn that the really of their two different personalities would not blend as one. Either way Allen needed to know. Seeing her in person would also dissolve any false sense of who she was that he may have acquired by getting to know from afar. He did know If anything was going to scare Doris away, this letter would do it. After he finished the letter, four drafts later he sent it on its way. His shaking hands were obvious but he knew he had done the right thing. Now all he could do is wait for her response.

Dear Doris,

If I was asked to write a Love story I do not believe that I could. The words in my head would not adequately express the story of true Love that I would want to portray. I now know in my heart that I have experienced true Love. Over the years I have believed that some things happen due to circumstances and other things were meant to be. Although in the past year since I have known you I have learned that some of the things that just happen, were meant to be as well.

Out of all the words that could be used to describe me I believe bold would be last in line. To be honest it scares me silly to write these words to you I fear that this words could push you away. I also knew that if one has experienced true love it's important to know if the feeling goes both ways. Doris, this is my request of you today. I feel the best way to know if what we share is real is to meet face to face once again. I would like to come visit you in Indiana.

When we first met, I told you that my parents kept the spark alive, despite the time they were apart. My hope is that our letters have carried on my parent's legacy, and the connection that we felt a year ago is still there today. I will wait for your response before I come.

Sincerely,
Allen

Doris held the letter in her hand, as she took a minute to consider the man she has gotten to know the tears began flow. It was here that she had asked herself if she really had fallen in love. She began to cry even more when she realizes she knew the answer. There was no doubt in that she was in love. Her only reserve was the anticipation of the events that her response would bring to pass. She was both laughing and crying at the possibility of what is ahead. Doris took a few minutes to dry her tears, then she composed yet another letter to Mr. Lane and sent it on its way.

It had been a week since Allen sent the letter to Doris.

He sat at the kitchen table holding the one she wrote in return, still unopened. He stared at it as if waiting would ensure that good news was inside. Don came in from the living room stopped for a moment and nodded his head. Don then sat across from him and after a moment asked him if was going to open it. They both continue to stare at it for moment or two more. Allen felt as though he has to work harder to take a breath, he finally opened the letter from Doris. He had kept most of the letters from her to himself but considering the amount of time He has been talking to Don about her in the last week, he reads this one aloud for Don to hear.

Dear Mr. Lane

I have to say that I was, rather intrigued by your last letter, as I looked back to the letters you have sent over the past year, I do not recall such a poetic talent as this one contained. To this, I have to say that I am a much luckier Gal than I thought I was before.

Allen stopped because of his tears, he then tried to start reading again but end up handing it to Don to finish, Don took the pages from him, and continued where Allen had left off. Despite the fact that he is crying as well.

The fact of the matter Mr. Lane I was actually relieved at your letter last week as much as I have enjoyed getting to know you as both a sincere and humorous man. With this, I look forward to meeting with you again in person in the days ahead.

Both Allen and Don look at each other with relief.

Don's mind stop wandering as he landed in the

makeshift runway of his backyard. When he finally made it to his house he found the answering machine blinking and the number on the on the bottom of the screen he recognized as his brothers. Seeing that there was 3 messages Don wasted no time returning his call.

INDIANA

Cloverdale Indiana

Allen hung up the phone turned to Doris and told her that his brother was on his way.

Doris started to cry and Allen hugged her as she told him how scared she was. Allen reassured her that the search team would find him and there was nothing they could do but wait. Allen then reminded Doris that Danny was a survivor and with all the snacks that she had packed the back pack of his that he will be set for a little while at least. Allen knew that Danny would see it as an adventure, and probably was having the time of his life.

A little more than a hundred miles away in a little town called Shadeland, Quinn and Laura Luster are in their living room talking about all the hay fields they own. They were getting older and were wondering how much longer they were going to able to carry on. Their Daughter Addison was now living on her own so everything that was going to be done was now up to them. Laura is tapping away on her knitting needles, while Quinn has a magnifying glass on his model airplane. Their cat Dixie was sitting in the empty chair on the other side of the room. Laura looked up as she heard the sound of an airplane that seemed to be approaching the front door.

Don had been flying all day and so far everything had gone as planned until he glanced at the storm cloud that was just ahead. He looked around below for a place to land. His eye caught what appeared to be an abandoned hay field. He knew that the clouds this thick were not going to take long to flood the sky. As Don made his descend he saw the lighting out of the corner of his eye. When he landed he stopped the engine about a hundred yards away from the Lusters front porch. After shutting down the controls he climbed out of his seat and headed towards Quinn and Laura who are standing just off their porch. As Don started to explain why he landed in their field he turned and pointed in the directing of the sky.

Quinn and Laura said nothing about the field. Their focus was the storm and making sure Don was ok. They invited him inside and after Don glanced at the damage his plane had done he followed through the front door. As Don walked in, he was thankful for the warmth and comfortable chair. he saw the Lusters house as a homey warm atmosphere. It was small but sufficient light colored chairs with afghans draped almost randomly gave it a complete look that reminded him of home.

Don wasted no time trying to figure out what he was going to do about getting to his brother's. He told the Lusters about his nephew and his need to get there as soon as he could. Quinn looked at Laura and then back at Don. He then told Don about his motor home. Their Winnebago had just been fixed up to be road worthy again, and they were looking for an opportunity to take it for a drive. Don did not want to take advantage of them and started to say no, but Laura cut him off. Don smiled and nodded his head then responded with a yes ma'am. Quinn then told him that he would actually be doing them a favor. He had just spent a fair amount of money to fix it up and then realized that he was not in good enough shape to travel any more. The only thing Quinn wanted in return was a good tune up and then they would call it even. Quinn then told Don to put His airplane in the barn and it would stay there as long as he needed it to. Don thanked the Lusters but feeling the burden of what is in Cloverdale, said he probably should get going pretty soon.

As Don was leaving the driveway he nodded his head and laughed out loud as he thought of Laura and Quinn and they're two totally different personalities. Laura was just as sweet as his mom's apple pie, but stood firm in what she believed. She insisted on Don borrowing the motorhome as well as his need for a box of fresh baked cookies and snacks. Quinn when he talked he got to the point, and made you stop and think.

As Don turned onto the highway he thought about the last thing Quinn had said. He told Don that he did not believe that people just fall out of the sky into their lives for no reason. He said you are family now so take the time you need but don't be a stranger. When you make it back and we will have a proper visit. Don reached over to the box of goodies that Laura fixed. When he did he noticed that the money that he had left for the Lusters was in the box as well. As he continued towards Allen's house his mind wandered back to the last time he came for Allen's wedding.

It was February 1971 the wedding was on the twenty eighth, and that was still several weeks away. As Allen and Don sat on the front porch Allen was telling Don about all that had to be done. Doris wanted to have a horse pull her up to the altar from the back field of their house. Her dad was building a platform with wheels on it that had two horses would pull with George and Doris on it. There was the tradition of using her mother's wedding dress, but she wanted cowboy boots as well. It reminded Don of something from biblical days. It also took him by surprise he did not see Doris as the outgoing adventure type. Allen had told him that it was what tipped the scale and made me fall head over heels for her. Allen then talked about the night he met Doris at the Lubbock fair. He said it was luck that she happen to come through town that night. Luck or fate there was no doubt in Allen's mind that she was the one.

Don pulled up to Allen's house and as he saw James with his head under the hood He wondered what it would have been like, had it been him that found the girl of his dreams. Allen and Don both believed they had found what they were looking for in life, although today Don thinks that Allen got a better deal. Don Did not know Doris all that well himself but Allen had once explained her as a gracious, amazing women, that was not only a magician in the kitchen but a great mom as well.

For Don it was relief to visit his Brother. Seeing Allen's family was always fun. Don would claim not having his own was the way he preferred it. But he did love visiting here and seemed to love it more every time he came. James looked up from the hood and his dad coming his way. He told Don that he had checked all the fluid levels he had told him to and was wondering what else to do. Don had a slight smirk but James was to focused to notice. He told him to start the truck up and they would see how it sounded. James jumped in the truck with excitement to turn the key, he then looked out the passenger window to see his dad is still in the house. After Don waved his hand James turned off the engine and returned to the front of the truck. Then said hi to his Uncle. James had never met Don, but he knew about him and well there's no mistaking the resemblance of Dads brother. James glanced back at the house to see Allen looking at him and gave him a smile and thumbs up.

Just them the radio that James had on his belt started to make some noise. James stepped away and put the radio up to his ear. Don watched James out of the corner of his eyes while his head was still under the hood. His curiosity got the best of him and he made his way over to where James was. When he got there James was busy telling some truckers how to save some tie getting off the highway. The part of town that James was leading them to was the downtown area of Cloverdale that had every shop imaginable, Walmart, Home Depot, target, etc. the place James had been specific talking about was a truck stop called Flying J's kind of like putting grocery store truck stop and clothing store in a blender and pouring it out over one city block.

When James was almost done talking to the trucker he caught a glance of the curious look in Don's eyes and gave him one in return.

Allen's Daughter Kathleen has been in a huff every scene she heard Don was coming. She had assumed until then that she was going with her Dad to look for Danny. As the oldest of the three kids she had always been the one to watch out for her younger brothers and now that Danny the youngest of the two was lost in the woods she was mad. So mad she was hotter that one momma's fresh baked sweet potatoes. As she paced the floor left and right with her arms folded in front of her she presented her case. She said if she could go down there she would give them a piece of my mind. What nerve they had to lose her little brother why can't they lose one of their own kids.

Allen and Doris were not sure what to say to Kathleen to ease her mind. They were rather touched to see how worried she was about her little brother. Kathleen's brown eyes and hair may have come from her father but the way she reacted to things came from her mother and Doris may had learned to temper her responded on the outside you can bet your next month paycheck that she was just as hot as Kathleen. Allen was worried as any father would be but he was trying to holding it together. The biggest reason why he asked his brother to come was he would need a shoulder to cry on. For now, he needed to stay strong for his family they were depending on him for support. James as the middle child he was not always sure which way he should to go. He was the second two oldest and second to the youngest. either way he was worried about Danny as well. While it was tempting to wearing a hole in the floor next to Kathleen, outside checking the fluids in the pickup seem to be that he needed to go.

Ten minutes later Allen and Don were looking at the map planning their route.

Don pointed to a spot on the map, and asked if it was the place they were going.

Allen nodded yes and said that it was small little town it was not easy to find but once you know where it is, it's just a matter of, getting there. Don then pointed to spot north and to the left on the map, then marks it with an X. Then Don explained the problem. He showed Allen the place where he landed in Shadeland. The storm he ran into was in a little town there. It was not showing much of a chance of stopping any time soon they're that close it's probably getting hit as well.

Allen grabbed the map and jumped up and Don followed him.

Allen then said goodbye to Doris and his kids and was out the door. The truck was loaded with enough camp equipment for a week. As they head out the door Allen put his hand on Don's shoulder. Allen says nothing at first but as the get in the cab of the truck Allen lets out a long sigh and thanked him for coming.

Don did not say anything in response but only nodded his head. That was enough of a response for Allen to know the he had heard him and was aware of how much emotion was behind the simple dialog

An hour later Don and Allen both jumped after bolt of lightning struck the road in front of them. The windshield wipers on were on the highest setting and Don was in the driver seat. His head was leaned up next to the windshield and Allen was in the same position acting as another set of eyes. Jonesville was still thirty minutes away but their speed for the last forty-five minutes was no more than twenty miles per hour.

They finally reach Jonesville and they pull into a Dinner just of the highway. A young lady in her forties was behind the counter and offered them coffee before the make it in the door. She did not wait for a response but had two cups poured by the time they reached the counter. When she saw that the sugar and cream was getting low she yelled for her son Walter. A heavy set short teen boy come from around the side of the counter. Emma motioned towards the counter where the coffee and cream was and Walter disappeared through the doorway with the bowls in his arm. Emma turned toward Don and Allen, her first question was why they were out in such a frightful storm. Both Don and Allen had their hands wrapped around their coffee cups. Allen explained that his son Danny was lost in the forest out there and he and his brother where there to help find him. He motioned to Don as he took a drink. Don then asked if she could tell them where to find the search party. When he was finished he saw the look in Emma's face.

She stood straight up her mouth went open and her hand went in front of it.

She then put her pointer finger up while reaching under the counter for the phone handset. A minute later the phone is in her ear. The conversation was quiet at first, until all the sudden she screamed out loud. Allen and Don look at each other and then laugh as they realize what was going on. Emma was chewed out her husband Harry for calling off the search due to the weather. Emma then pointed out how wet and cold the little ten-year-old boy was, and that he would be getting off his precious recliner to come get Allen and Don. She slammed the receiver down and turned back to them. She said that her husband would will be right here to get them, and they will not rest until their boy was found. Allen and Don both tip their cowboy hats and more water drains to the floor.

Ten minutes later the glare of the headlights shined through the side window of the dinner. It was not quite night yet but the storm cloud was making it look as it was. Don and Allen begin the process of putting on their coat and boots while Emma stood in the view of the window giving her husband, the glare. Harry sat in the cab of truck looked back at her with somewhat of a guilty grin, then tipped his hat at her. Allen climbed in the cab with Harry and Don follow behind in the truck they brought from Cloverdale. They Drove down several windy roads towards the camp site. The rain was beginning to let up but they still were taking it slow because of the water on the roads. They stopped at a clearing on the side of the road close to camp site where he was lost.

There were twelve guys, they took a few minutes to go over the game plan and break up into groups. There were dirt pathways and information signs in various places. Danny had wondered off the trail several times. When the storm came in is when he got lost. Everyone was given a radio and a flash light. Three blinks of the flashlight was the signal that Danny was found. Allen and Don were in separate groups because of their lack of knowledge of the area. The storm came and went in intensity and the crashes of thunder still happened at a moment's notice. Harry and Don head out to the forest.

They reached a point where several bushes would hide the four-foot drop offs. This could easily spook and injure a ten-year-old. The canal was a fun place to hide for kids and is also somewhat shielded from the weather.

As Don and Harry started to talk Don learned the Jonesville had always been a small town and one of the reasons why they set up the summer camp was to reach out to other towns nearby. It was slow at first. Now the applications come from all over Indiana. This year they had the population of Jonesville doubled.

Don then told Harry about growing up in Lubbock and the events leading up to coming here.

Harry asked him how long he had been a pilot Don told him ten years. Then Don said it had been his dream since he was eighteen and told him about the time he saw the airplane at the county fair in Lubbock. When Allen moved away and got married he just needed something to focus on. So after a year or so of the different textbook and practical test he had his license and was looking for plane to fly.

They had made their way out in the woods enough now that the flash lights were more of an asset to them that the search lights at the beginning of the trail. It was starting to get cold but they were determined because of the mission at hand. Don looked up as the rain started up again. He peaked around the bushes and trees as they came and went alone the path.

Don stopped and pulled his foot out of a branch that had been intertwined with a tree root bulging up from the ground. Conversations had stopped and started several times as they focused on the forest. They periodically yelled out Danny's name. At times they could hear in the distance the other groups doing the same. Other times however it was all they could do to hear one another.

Harry at one point asked if there were other siblings beside Allen and him. Don said that because his parents had two at one time that he thought it might have been all they could handle. Then he added that they were a handful to raise. As they went along Harry pointed out the places he knew were danger spots hidden by bushes. They continued to look behind bushes and under the cliff over hangs. The lighting continued to strike. The storm was now drowning out everything but the sound of Don voice. As the radio started to squeal Don would put it up to his ear.

Don turned when the lighting bolted behind him as he did he lost his footing and slid in one of the mud puddles the next thing he knew he was on the ground sliding down one of the slopes. Harry had been right behind him and yelled down to make sure he was alright he then offer him a branch to pull him up. Don, now caked in mud got himself up and was looking at the area he had fallen into. He decided that this was as good of a place as any to resume his search. He brushed to the extra mud off. Then stood gave Harry a thumbs up and continued his search from where he was. The ground was uneven but Don was taking it slow anyway he was trying to make sure that he did not miss any potential hiding places. Several hours had passed since the search began. For the guys out searching it was hard to tell what time it really was. No one was taking time to look at a watch and it was too dark to see one anyhow. There was no time to be tired and none of them showed that they were.

As Don moved down the narrow path he looked under everything in his way. With several hours of not finding anything he was starting to think about whether he need to search another area, until he found what he hoped was a break in his luck. He had found what appeared to be a dried up water canal. He yelled up to Harry then keyed up the radio to confirm that his message had gotten across. The size of the hole was a little tight for Don but for Danny was probably a comfortable fit. So Don made his way in he noticed the temperature in the cave had to be at least five or ten degrees warmer and it was a perfect place for a kid to hide from the rain. Inside it was larger than he thought it would be there was almost enough room to pull his thermos out. He did take a moment to warm his hands but then made his way further in. As he moved could hear the creak of the gravel and dirt above him. The thunder at one point seemed to shake the ground, Don could feel the tremble. Don was in good shape but it was difficult to see from side to side but he made each turn of his head count kicking the walls as he passed to make sure make sure no one was there.

As he made it further in he took a look around, he was little upset that all his crawling had so far had turned up no results he thought he had he wasted his time. Don even started to wonder if Danny had already been found and he missed it. However, he had been talking to Harry on the radio the whole time so he would have known if that was the case. He stopped and took a minute stretched, trying to work a cramp out of his leg. It was here that his eyes widened almost in disbelief.

Danny was laying on the ground only three feet from him. He had his backpack open and all the rappers from the cookies and crackers were scattered around him. It was hard to tell in the dark but it appeared that Danny was unharmed and asleep, as the snoring nostrils would suggest.

Don called out to Danny several times slapped his cheeks a then shook him a bit Danny moaned as he woke. Don started to get a rope out of his bag to pull Danny out. He stopped when he heard Danny's voice calling him dad. Don started to correct Danny's mistake but then decided to just to avoid it for now until he found out the extent of his injuries. Don told him to lay still and they would be out of there soon. Danny said he was hungry but tired as well.

Don call Harry when he first found the Danny but the radio did little good this far in the cave so he crawled back to the opening to signal to the group that Danny was ok. When he reached the place where he had come in, he realized that the opening had caved in and they were stuck inside. Harry had gone to signal the rest of the group that Danny was found so all Don could do was wait. With the rain still at its peak the search party was now converted into a rescue mission. Don had made several attempts to reopen the hole but had learned that it was to solid to do without a shovel and was no use. Danny had been coming more alert and was now talking with Don none stop. Danny said he thought his dad was joking when he talked about his twin.

Danny squinted and turned his head as he looked at Don. Don assured him that his dad was not joking and he did have a twin

Danny stares for another minute to decide if Don was telling the truth or not.

Don then pulled his bag over and ruffles though to the bottom retrieving a sandwich inside. Don hands it to him and asked if he like card games. Danny said he just liked to build houses and Don pulls a deck out of his bag. They use a clearing on the ground and started to build one together.

The Laughter from Danny was a relief to Don. As they took turns making additions to their structure Don again fumbled through his bag this time for the spare Batteries to his flashlight.

As The canal went dark Danny Grab his leg and grip it tight. When the light went back on Danny started looking through his bag and pulling out another snack before drifting off to sleep.

THE RESCUE

While Don is waiting he thought about Danny and the family life he has. Over the years Don had progressively given up on family life he argued that he was ok alone. The question was however, was he really. Danny was awake again and had been staring at Don. He was still trying to figure out what was the difference between His Uncle and His Dad but he finally gave up gain. he instead started asking his question of Don. Was he really a piolet and if so did he wear the goggles and scarf and ride one of those planes that looks like a cannon with two holes in it. Don laughs at Danny's description of an airplane. He then told him that his plane is one you get inside and has doors like a car. Don started to tell the story of when he used to pretend he was flying one of those like in the old snoopy cartoon. Danny however finished the ending and then said his Dad had told him that one as well.

Don nodded his head then lifted his eyebrow

Danny continued and said back in the old days when he thought Dad his was joking about having a twin he would hear stories about his Dad growing up in Texas. Don laughed at Danny's back in the old day's comment. Danny then said that it had been two whole months since his Dad told him a story and he was a lot younger then.

Don asked him how he like being the youngest and

he said that his sister took good care of him and his mom helped some as well. James always did a lot of cool things with him and his dad was always telling him he was not really the youngest. Their dog's Clyde and pumpkin where both four and he was six years older than them.

Don heard a banging on the roof of the cave and the obvious sound of footsteps.

He crawled to where the opening had been and told Danny to yell real loud. Danny said he could sing louder than I can yell. Don then told him he could sing instead.

Don got to wall and started to bang, while Danny is singing at the top of his lungs.

Up top Allen heard the faint sound of Danny's voice. He put his hand up yelled for everyone to be quiet. He then jumped down to the grown and pressed his ear to the dirt.

Still focused he moved to a different spot but puts his hand up trying to keep everyone quiet. Then he heard it loud and clear. Danny was singing at the top of his lungs, the Jeff Barry song, Do wah ditty. As Allen got up he is both laughing and crying at the same time. And said it was the last time he would get on to him for singing to loud. Harry then handed Allen his radio, and took a shovel to the ground on the other side Don heard the thud. He then turned around putting his boots toward the wall and kicks with all his might. Allen key up the radio to try to reach Don, as he did about six shovels begin to penetrate the ground. Don slid back to protect Danny from the dust and debris.

Allen's emotion had been forcefully put on hold focusing all his energy at the entrance of the cave. When he saw Danny coming out of the hole lying on his back, he could not help himself he was in tears. Allen gave a nod to Don who had just come out himself then turned to his son to see if he was alright. He gave Danny a visible once over and there were no apparent bruises or cuts and other that one dirty kid he seemed to be just fine. Don and Danny both spent an hour in the ambulance but both road to the diner in pickup trucks.

At seven in the morning the Diner was usually crawling with folks wanting their breakfast. This morning however the diner had been closed because of the search, and was now getting ready to serve the disaster relief crew. When Emma heard the trucks pull into the lot. She began another pot of coffee then turn to the stove where the eggs, grits, bacon, sausage gravy and biscuits were being born. She yelled for Walter to start serving coffee and tea to everyone.

His head dropped and his face went into somewhat of a pout because he had just put his sweatshirt on to go and jump thru the puddles with his friends. She then pointed out that if he asked his friends to help he still might have some time later. She then reminded him that these guys have been out all night while he was under his nice warm quilt. Walter did not say anything, but the thought of the cold ground replacing his fuzzy pillow and his monster bear gave him the chills.

For the next hour Walter and his friends circled the diner. They refilled coffee cups took the plates to and from the tables and told to tell everyone that their meals were on the house.

When one of the boy's head heard this he was wondering If there were tables on the roof?

As time went on more plates made it to the dish sink and the sound of the chat began to rise. Don glanced to the corner of the room and spotted the pay phone.

He then pointed in the direction of the rectangle booth and Allen slid out of the chair and head that general direction, stopped for a moment looked back. Then brought Danny with him to call home. As the phone came alive Kathleen ran across the living room and into the kitchen. She had grabbed the handset before Doris had time to turn her head. The tears start to roll down from Kathleen's eyes when she realized it was Danny on the other end. It did not take her long to figure out that he was alright, as he is going on about all that he had been doing in the last week. Kathleen put the phone on speaker and Doris began to cry as well. They all listen more intently as Danny told them how much they would not believe the fun he was having.

Danny first told them he came in second place in the pie eating contest. Then he talked about exploring adventure and how he got lost in an underground cave. Uncle Don had come to find him. He thought it was Dad at first. He asked Kathleen is she knew that dad had a twin. He went on to say the door got stuck and they had spent the night and then Dad was there in the morning.

Kathleen put the phone on speaker and they were all laughing and crying.

He also told them about the Stethoscope that the paramedics used and how cold it was. Danny asked if his mom was there. Doris spoke up through her laughter to let him know she was listening. Then he told her that The restaurant that we are at has the best cinnamon rolls but their grits did not have any cheese. Doris promised to make some cheesy grits when he came home and asked for Allen to be put on the phone. Danny handed the receiver to Allen and went back to the table with Don. Doris took the phone off speaker and put the hand set to her ear.

Doris asked Allen if Danny was ok and Allen told her that he thought the whole thing was just part of the fun weekend and he did not have a scratch on him. While they were chatting Danny sat next to Don and put his fist on the table to challenge him at rock paper scissors. Don put his fist down as well and just as they are finishing the tie breaker round Allen was standing beside them. He said the Mom, bub, and Sissy were glad to hear from them and they had better get going to be in time for mom's special dinner.

When Danny heard that his mom was cooking he jumped out of his chair leaving his sweater behind. Before Allen and Don left their seats he was out the door and in the truck. Don and Allen laugh as they walk out themselves. Allen had grabbed the sweater they both gave their thanks to Harry and Emma as the walk pass the counter. As Allen walked out he the front door he was glad for the feeling of a weight lifted from his shoulders and they were out the Door and on the road by ten o'clock.

Doris and Kathleen were busy making sure that the guys welcome was the best it could be. They were planning a large country steak meal with the famous banana split cake for dessert. Kathleen, was making a special bowl of cheese grits for Danny. Doris knew her way around the stove, and she was never afraid to prove it. Her pink apron was now covered in flour from the biscuits. After she put the floured tray in the oven, she began to stir the gravy. Kathleen, eager to learn to cook like her mom was there following her every move

With Doris cooking had always been a way of showing her love especially when it was to her own family, thus every meal became a feast.

Don, Allen and Danny came out of the Seven eleven with their hostess cherry pies still hot from the microwave. To the Lane boys Cherry pies had never been about hunger it was just they were so good they always had room despite how many meals were in anticipated for the day. Danny and Allen both had been telling Don of the great wonders that Doris's Kitchen could produce and in Don's mind it was like the memory growing up with his Grandma Laura all over again. After the breakfast they had at the diner in Jonesville some would wonder how there was room for another feast in the same day. Those who wondered however had not tasted the cooking of Doris Lane

As they reach the fence line of Allen's property Danny's attention is turned to his dogs. After about three minutes of Danny's Excitement Don stopped to let him run with the dogs. As they continue towards the house Don slowed more to give Danny the feeling of being in the lead. Don also wants to make sure he can see the dogs running along the side of him. He drove for a bit more then stopped the truck, honked the horn and yelled to Danny to jump in the back. Danny protested that he was winning and Allen agreed with him and told him that was why it was not a fair race.

Allen and Don laugh as Danny hoped in the back of the pickup. On the way to the house Don asked Allen if his wife's cooking was as good as he had made it out to be. Don Made an abrupt stop and looked at him with disbelief. Better than Grandma Laura, that was not possible. But it was what Allen had said. Soon enough Don would find out for himself. Allen glanced back to make sure Danny did not fall out of the truck. Then told Don about southern fried steak that melted in your mouth. There was also her country gravy, mash potatoes, and biscuits, well let's just say if Allen ever have to go on a diet he will be in trouble.

Don stopped in front of the house no sooner did he get the truck in park and Kathleen, Doris and James were running out of the house to greet them. Allen and Don are almost run over by Kathleen trying to get to Danny. When Don stepped onto the porch he took a sniff of the meal cooking inside and he knew that Allen was telling the truth about how good Doris was in the kitchen.

It did not take long for Kathleen and James to get all the details from Danny of his great adventures at camp Jonesville. Both Dogs had climb the steps of the porch and have done somewhat of a plop into their beds. Don and Allen were both getting the finger pointed eye roll from Doris for snitching a taste of the gravy before it was done. As the two brothers stood together is was easy to see that identical was an understatement both brown hair brown eyes and as Kathleen walked by them she noticed that even the mole on her Dad's left ear was in the same place on her uncle.

Danny's first question to his mom was he wanted to know what was for desert. Kathleen's question to him was How could he be sure that she is making one. Danny was not fooled he knew his mom always had something sweet in her dinner plan. There was a moment of silence and Kathleen motioned towards the stove where the pot of grits was cooking along with the bowl of cheese on the counter beside. Danny's eyes widened and he licked his lips.

Allen, Doris, and Don sat at the kitchen table while the Three kids took their plates to the front porch.

Now that the all the commotion was starting to settled down Allen and Doris asked Don, who the people were that loaned him the motor home. Don recapped the adventure of having to land the plane in a hurry, then told them that he felt as they basically took him in as the son they never had. They did not say a word about the fact that he had ruined their field, instead they invited him to lunch. Quinn had a very dry humor but he also had a way of finding out what you needed and just taking care of it weather you liked it or not. Laura she said was very giving and caring at heart. She however would not take no for an answer no matter what it was. If she thought, for example that you need a shoe box full of snacks you were not leaving without then.

Despite their persistence that Don had done them no harm, he thought he need to find a way to repay them somehow. Not only did he use their hay field for a runway but it looked as though he could do some chores for them when he took the motor home back. Don nodded his head as he got up for a serving of grits Danny did not finish, he then topped it with some gravy from the stove. The only thing they asked for in return is to give their motor home a tune up. The other thing the Lusters said was they wanted him to bring the family with him when he came back. Both Allen and Doris nod their heads and mouth the word wow to each other. Don began to stare at the arrangement of family pictures and for a moment is lost in thought.

Don was back at the table with Doris and Allen. He dropped his tone and he posed the next phrase as more of a question. Quinn said one thing that he did not know what to do with.

He said they did not believe that people just drop out of the sky for no reason he was family now. Don did not know whether to thank him for being so nice or laugh because I did actually fall out of the sky. The thing that made Don stop and think was he knew that Quinn meant what he said. They were all silent for a few minutes pondering the moment until Doris spoke up.

Doris was having no talk about going anywhere. They had all had a very long emotional couple days and what they needed was a good night sleep before anything else. She got up and started to clear the dishes. Allen knocked on the screen separating them from the front porch and Kathleen, James and Danny came in from outside.

James was sent to help Danny get his bag unpacked Kathleen went to check on her Grandpa.

As Kathleen turned to leave she had this uneasy feeling about Don. He was again focused on the photos on the wall but he had somewhat of a heavy look in his face. It seemed to be almost silently yell. Kathleen pondered this as made her way out the door but Allen had caught the look in her eyes and had wondered what was going on.

Allen, Doris and Don did the dishes and wiped the table, while the coffee was brewing. Danny ran out in his pajamas just as the cake was being sliced, James followed shortly behind. While Danny's entrance was an enthusiastic run anticipating the cake that was being served. James was at a slower place thinking about what was on the other end of his hand held radio. He walked out the front door the and squeal of the radio caught Dons ear. Don looked at Allen and pointed with obvious interest. He motioned with his hands and Don followed James out the door. As Don walked out he saw the hand held radio up at his ear while he tried to make out the voice on the other end. While they are talked about radios, Allen and Doris talk about how easy their sons had taken to their Uncle in such a short time. They also wondered why Kathleen was reacting to him. It was not something either Allen or Doris wanted to deal with at the time and were hoping that the it was just a result of the stress of the last couple days and would resolve itself it due time. the whole family turn early exhausted from the emotion of the day.

LIFE ON FARM

Don had never been able to sleep late, growing up as a farmer had him getting up early, and it just became a habit that he never let go of. As he laid in the bed of the motor home he tried to convince himself that he did not need to be awake but finally he gave in. He turned on the coffee pot and dresses for his jog. When Allen and him moved the motorhome to the side of the house he took note of a dirt road just beyond the front porch it would be a good place to get some exercise as well as explore his brothers land. As he tied his shoes the smell of the coffee tempted him but he knew he would enjoy it more after his jog. He walked down the steps and began to run in place to warm up. He looked in the direction of the house he saw his brother with the dogs, on the front porch. Allen spoke first.

He started with some harassment about sleeping in. Then he said he would show him around, if he could manage to keep up. Don assured Allen that the only reason he was not going to leave him in the dust was he was the tour guide. They both took off jogging at a steady pace with Pumpkin and Clyde by their side despite the harassment that they tossed each other, they kept in stride with one another throughout the jog. Their conversation started with the lay of the land, a progressed from there to memories of the years gone by.

The last time Don had come was Allen's wedding more than ten years ago. There was a lot of talk about landscaping and as Allen pointed to the hay field on either side of the road it was two square miles. He then said that part was originally plowed by Doris's great grandfather years ago. Don nodded his head and pointed to a house in the distance that had just became visible as they ran parallel with another field. It was a small house painted blue and white. Allen picked up a tennis ball and through it in the direction of the house and Pumpkin ran after it.

Allen told him that Doris's Dad George lived out there. He had been there ever since the deed to the property got transferred. A couple years ago they tried to get him to move closer to the house, but he would not budge. He was kind of a keep to yourself guy. Don recalled that he had seen a clearing of land near the house. Doris and Allen latter decided to send Kathleen back their couple days at a time every week, just to make sure he is ok. They do send her with a chore list that she would rather not have, but she does enjoy the fact that they are letting her branch out. It gave her a sense of independence and responsibility.

Don and Allen have now turned the corner and were headed back in the direction of the house. Pumpkin is again by their side and he had dropped the ball at Don's feet and had an expected look on his face. Allen said that it would only take one time and he would have a friend for life. Don had always wanted a dog but never got around to getting one. A smile cracked on his face, he then picked up the ball reached his arm and leg back as a pitcher with a baseball and threw it as far as he could. Pumpkin darted off after it while Clyde is still keeping stride with them. Allen does not quite know if Clyde is lazy or just like the companion status of being with him but he usually just sticks close.

On the way back to the house they continued to discuss different things. Don had asked how old his kids were now and he said Danny was ten James was twelve and Kathleen was thirteen. Allen went on to say that ever since Kathleen had turned twelve that all the rules had changed.

They are on the porch now, Clyde has returned to his blanket, and Pumpkin is now hovering over Clyde apparently trying to encourage him that it is not time go to bed again. Clyde does not seem convinced.

Allen was wondering how long they had run and looked at his watch. It was almost seven forty-five. They had been running for more than an hour. In all the years That he had known Doris her meal times have never varied eight o'clock on the weekends and summer and seven when kids are in school. Allen told Don this as he starts towards the camper to cleaned up.

Before he got away Allen yelled after him and told him he could use the bathroom in the house.

Don thought about the fact that he was using the Luster's camper. They did say to feel free to use the shower, however he thought that one less time might be better. Don nodded his head and returned a few minutes' latter with his clean clothes a towel. He was also carrying a pot of coffee as well. He walked in the house and Allen is eating a piece of crisp bacon, as Don passes he grabs one of his own then makes his way to the bathroom, leaving the coffee pot behind.

When Don returned, Doris and Allen have finished half of the coffee. Doris was pouring pancake batter on the stove and Allen was searching the fridge for the orange juice. They were in the middle of a conversation about Danny. He was having nightmare about monsters from the woods. Every time he got afraid or has a traumatic experience he has the nightmares.

When Don heard them talking he asked Allen if have tried their Dads old technique. Allen just stared trying to recall what he was referring to. Don waited a few minutes to see if he was going to remember, then told the story. When they were eight, Allen used to get bad nightmares somehow their dad came up with this little rhyme to help him and it made Don laugh as well. Don waited again to see if Allen was going to recall what he was talking about. Finally, he said that after they said good night to him he would try their Dads trick on him. Allen and Doris both look at each other and pause. They were of course looking for anything that would help Danny.

That night Don took his place in his favorite chair to wait for Allen and Doris as they said good night. After they were done Allen motioned towards Danny's bedroom and Don made his way in. Both Doris and Allen were still wondering what Don had up his sleeve but were eager to explore anything that would help Danny. As Don makes his way to Danny's bed Allen and Doris take their place on the porch swing.

Don is hoping that he can remember the funny little saying that his dad quoted all those years ago. He had jotted down what he could recall that morning and was going to have to make up the rest. The first question Don had for Danny was he wanted to know if the monsters were the funny ones or the scary ones. Danny assured Don that the monsters he saw were the scary ones. Danny was rather surprised at the question. He was unaware that the funny monsters even existed. Don started to tell him about Casper the ghost but decided to move on with his dad's little story instead. Don said that he might have a way to convince him that not all monsters were bad. Danny did not say anything and Don continued. He was now using a higher pitch voice to lighten Danny's mood.

There is a monster in my bed and he is stomping on my feet. Don was using his fist to make Danny's bed bounce. The monster I hear interrupts my sleep, but I'm not scared he is a cuddly guy soft and furry and wears a tie. At this point Don shows Danny the stuffed animal that he had been hiding, it looks similar to a monster but was now wearing the bright colored tie. It did not take long for Danny to rescue the stuffed animal for his pillow. He slips in at night and tells a joke or two then he asks for a bite of my snack when I'm through. As the night goes on, we laugh more and more, then I realize I'm not scared like before. So if you're up at night and can't go to sleep. Or you're getting stepped on by your monster's feet. Just remember yours is cuddly too and he probably just wants to snuggle with you.

Doris and Allen's curiosity had got the best of them and they had been listening outside Danny's door almost since the beginning of Don's story. As soon as they realize that Don is about to be done with Danny, they quickly retreat to the living room. By the time Don was done Danny was laughing and telling Don how funny it was. Danny then asked if he could sleep with his monster for the night. Don told him to just hang on to him for a bit to make sure the mean monsters don't come back. As Don came into the living room Allen and him exchange a glance and he sat in the chair across from them. Allen still did not recall his Dad coming up with such things. Don then said it might have been mom. Don then reminded him that they were always coming up with these rhyming twerks to help them remember things. Allen did recall that.

THE DECISION

It was time for Don to start making plans to finish his commitments in Indiana so he could get back to his routine in Lubbock. The job that he had with the resort in Lubbock was unpredictable, so the pager he carried was The only communication they had. Despite he had let them know he would be out of town for a period of time the pager had gone off several times while he was there in Indiana. The agreement he had was a freelance job. It however was now the biggest bread winner he had.

He started by tell Allen that he going to have to get on his way the next day. He started to talk about the repairs on the Lusters farm as well as what was waiting for him in Lubbock. Allen and Don had walked outside, and were walking the path in front of the house. Allen told him he did not have to leave and he could stay for a while. It had been nice being able to catch Don thought. He then held up the pager and told Allen that duty was calling him home. Allen then reminded Don about the promise he had made. Don had told Allen and Doris that the next time he went to the Lusters he was going to bring his family. He did not want to admit it but he knew he had been duked by his own words.

They had just stepped into the camper and were resting on the couch inside. It had been a busy couple days

Don was starting to believe a day or two to unwind would be good. He did need to call the resort to let them know He had not forgotten them He would do that tomorrow. Right now he need to sleep. He told Allen as much, turned and went to the bed in the back. He was asleep almost before Allen made it out the door.

Allen walked into the living room he sat in his chair to read the paper. Doris was sitting across from him on the phone. He couldn't quite make out what she was saying but as he glanced at her from time to time he noticed her facial expressions had gone from confused and surprised, to excited and silently crying. Allen continued to watch and he began to read less of the paper and listen more to Doris. She replaced the reciver and Allen folded the newspaper and gave his full attention to her.

She told him that she had been taking to her Uncle. They both were silent for a moment.

Allen was a little puzzled because he did not recall Doris Having mentioned an Uncle before.

Doris responded to his expression by telling him about her Mom and Uncle David and how inseparable they were. Together as kids they loved everything from beach boys to beetles. Doris's Mom was the host of a family barbecue every weekend of the year. Uncle David did not have a family of his own so he was always there as well. Looking back Doris was sorry that he had never married but recalled that he was there to help her with her teenage year more than she might have realized. They were also times when she was just as mad at him as she was at her Dad. When her Mama died they all took it hard. The best part was Uncle David stepped in and provided that emotional support that they all needed. Uncle David never had been the one to ask for help for himself.

He was so busy being an emotional pillow to Doris and George that it was hard to tell that he was slipping away himself. He at one point decided that he need to get away. When he did he made it sound kind of mysterious. He was going out on an adventure not sure where he was going to land. Despite the promises that he made to stay in contact this is the first Doris had heard from him since the day he left.

David had been trying to get ahold of them for the last two years. However, because he did not leave the telephone number or forwarding address they could not let him know when they move from Mexia. James and Kathleen had come in and reached in the cupboard for the Chex mix then make their way to the table James grabbed a bowl full while Kathleen was waiting her turn.

Allen asked if Danny had gone to sleep yet Kathleen told him that he was snoring away with his head buried in Uncle Don's blue monster. Doris continued by tell Allen how deep her Uncle's voice sounded on the other end of the phone. She had always thought of him of having such soft tone about him.

When Doris had asked David where he had been all this time. He told her that for the last several years he had been in Mexia looking for them, and before that had been moving around depending on where the work took him. He then made a joke about the old Beach boys song, I get around. She then to him about finding the land in Indiana when she was nineteen and how the whole move came about. She also told him about Allen and their kids. This had gone on for hour. As Doris was telling Allen all this she first started to laugh and then began to cry as well. The last thing she said in between her yawns was that she had given him their address and she was wondering what was going to happen next. Then before Allen had time to escort her to bed she was asleep on the couch. Allen fluffed the pillows and laying a quilt over her. He then tiptoed out of the room motioning to James and Kathleen to do The same.

ADDISON

Quinn and Laura heard the sound of the car outside. A moment later their daughter walked in the front door. As she made her way into the living room she began to feel at ease. For thirty years Addison knew that this place had been a strong source of comfort. It was not only the house she grown up in but it was the warm feeling of love that she felt as she grew. It had been several years since she had actually lived there but every time she walked through the door it felt as she was coming home. She could smell her mom's cooking from the porch and stopped a moment to take it all in. As Addison walked in and asked what had happened to the field on the back end of the house.

Laura told her that a young man been there and had to land his airplane because of a storm.

Addison's ears perked up when she heard what Laura was saying. Laura them said that he was trying to get to his brothers so they had loaned him the motor home. Addison asked where his plane was and when Laura said it was in the barn without a word Addison turned and flew out back to meet up with Quinn. She found her Dad in the barn admiring the airplane, for a moment she just watched him. She pondered the idea of how she ended up with such great parents. When Quinn heard her running across the gravel He looked over to saw his daughter. He knew what she was going to ask the moment he saw the look in her eyes. Before she had a chance to say anything he told her that his name was Don Lane and he was in his mid-thirties. After that he said something that made the butterfly's in her stomach do another flip. He told her that she could meet him herself when he came back. Addison looked up with an excited grin on her face and asked when he was coming. Quinn told he that when he came though he did not know exactly how long of a visit it was going to be. They did tell him to take as long as he need. He would at some point come back for his plane.

Back at Allen's house Kathleen came in the door and her face brightened and she made her way over to her dad to give him a hug. On her way to her mom she asked if lunch was ready. Danny jumped up out of his chair and ran over to grab Kathleen's legs to hug her.

After this Danny went into the living room and in the cupboard under the coffee table was the where all his cards were. They were the discarded mismatch decks that Doris had used over the years. He had learned that card houses were a fun pastime and Doris had learned that it would keep him occupied for hours. After he ate the sandwich Doris had made he started to build one across the floor. Then started another and looped it around the back of the table. It was no wonder that he earned the name the card house king.

Their living room was small but homey one couch one Loveseat and two chairs and a large pillow that Danny loved to sit on. The coffee table and two end tables always had bowls of candy one then. On the far wall was a small frame that held the ice cream sundae tickets that Allen had won at the fair when they met. The plan for the afternoon was the girls were going do some shopping in town while the guys held down the fort at home. Doris looked at the clock and started to clear the table. Don and Allen look up from there magazines, and look at each other.

James is busy making a list of things he is going to buy after he starts his new job. Allen pushed his shoulder and used hand motion to encourage him to help. James got up both Allen and Don did as well.

Allen took the dishes out of Doris's hand and Don did the same to Kathleen. Doris tried to take care of it but both of them were firm that they were going to take over and it was time for the girls go have their fun. Doris still resisted but Allen and Don both made it clear that they had it covered. The kitchen was officially off limits to them. She finally gave up and submitted as her and Kathleen went to get ready for their day. The guys then commenced with the cleanup job.

Doris walked past to go out the door and it appeared that there was a bigger mess than when she had left.

When the girls went to town Kathleen talked about her getting a driving lesson. Doris gave her a surprised look and Kathleen said that she was fifteen and only a year away from driving age. She then said that she was going to drive her Dads car Doris turns and looks at her again this time she pulled to the side of the road. The idea that Allen was going to let Kathleen drive his pink Cadillac was in Doris's mind, not going to happen. The fact of the matter was he did not let anyone drive his car. He himself had not even driven it since he brought it home. Kathleen was sure that her father was going to give into her when she asked him. She had always been able to sweet talk her way into anything with her dad. If the sweet talking did not work she would bring out her secret weapon, the puppy dog eyes.

They drove into the parking lot of the Dairy Queen made their way in and found a seat. While they waited Kathleen asked why her dad had the pink Cadillac Doris told her that when her Grandparents moved to Dallas her Dad and uncle both wanted to take the pink Cadillac family cookie jar. There was a debated on the why each of them should have the cookie jar. They did everything from rock paper scissors to all night monopoly game each time with the cookie jar in the pot each time her Uncle would win it her dad would win it back. Each time bragging about what they were going to use it for. The ice cream Sundays they had ordered were brought to them.

Kathleen was still wondering why was there such a tug a war. Doris told her that before it was her grandma's it was her great grandma's, and her Dad and uncle Don spent their childhood taking cookies out of it. When it came time to pass it on they both argued that because they thought they had taken the most cookies that it was rightly theirs. This was the biggest debate of all.

What Doris heard was during one of the ongoing arguments about who had eaten the most cookies Allen had made a comment that he had eaten enough cookies to fill a real Cadillac. Don then said if he could find a real Cadillac he will give him this one to match it. So don kept the cookie jar. Then Allen took it upon himself that he was not going to be beat. He went about the business about finding one a Cadillac.

They finished their Sundays and headed out the door to begin their chores. First was the grocery store. They needed pork chops. for dinner. Dr. pepper for Allen and Don and Whoppers for Danny's cake. Doris used Dr, pepper for the pork chops as well. Dr pepper chop she called them. Kathleen started asking questions about her mom's recipes and where they had all come from. Doris told her that her Dads mom gave many of them to her at their wedding and serval of them she had come up herself.

Kathleen loved her role as the oldest sibling she had many times been counted on as more than just a sister. She was a baby sister when mom's birthday and anniversary came around. Protector when Danny was being bullied. She was there with a bandage when James would scrape his knee and her favorite part was the party planner for all the birthdays and the twentieth of May it would be Danny's big day.

They pulled into the parking lot of the grocery store and Kathleen started asking questions. The first thing she asked was how her dad purposed to her mom. She imagined him down on one knee holding he moms hand. Doris told her that he did get on one knee but it wasn't quite as smooth as she might of thought. There was a hesitation long enough for Kathleen to wonder where the rest of the story was. Kathleen finally rolled her arm in a circle to encourage Doris.

Doris began again as they are walking down the aisle searching for their list. Allen had written some of the most beautiful poetry she had ever read when they were dating. However, when he got ready to ask the question his romantic juices floated away. Doris said he might have been busy winning a pie eating contest when those lessons were taught. Kathleen put a pack of Dr. pepper in the cart. She then laughed, remembering the story she had heard about how her parents met. When Allen had it figured out that they were a sure thing I guess he did not see the need for the formalized proposal.

He was right they were both head over heels in love. The first time Doris saw him dump his face in that pie she was convinced. It is every girl's dream to have a man propose and Doris's dad was not about let it be done any way other than the proper way. Doris had overheard Allen and George talking she almost ran up to join them until she heard what they were saying.

He was asking George permission to propose to Doris. When she heard him ask that question. She thought about how uncommon those kind of proper etiquette manners of getting permission from the father for a marriage proposal. George liked things just a certain way. So he was happy to see that Allen had come to ask, but the happiness ended when he asked about how he was going to ask her. He was going to go find her and ask her right away.

George's head went up and his hands went out in front of his body and he was standing at attention. Before Allen had a chance to get away George stopped him and said that they need to have a little chat. George took him by the shoulder and they walked down the path.

Doris would have loved to follow them but she did not. If Allen had asked her without the formalities, she would've said yes. But when a man goes to all the trouble to make a proposal an event it gives a woman the security that they will be taken care of in life.

They left the parking lot and headed towards home as they passed the Dairy Queen the conversation started again. Doris told Kathleen about the dinner in Mexica that she went to when she wanted to be alone. There were times as a teenager that she missed her momma so much that she just needed to go to a place that was familiar. Doris then told her of shopping days with her mom and the fun they had together when she was a kid. Kathleen waited patiently as Doris dabbed a tissue on her eyes. Then Doris told her about a childhood experience that made them both cry.

Doris had just turned fourteen. The hospital didn't always let kids her age go to the birthing center but Doris had that same sweet talking charm that Kathleen claimed to have with her Dad, so they let her come in. The first part was just like at home. Her mom Debbie was in her pajamas doing the breathing exercises that she had been doing for months. Doris did not understand much of the rest of what was happening. She did remember that at one point her mom was having trouble breathing at that point George and her were ushered out by the nurse.

George went and sat on the chair in the hall. He normally would put up a fight before he just succumbed to sitting and waiting, while his wife was in need of attention. This time he just gave in. Doris sat by her Dad for a bit but later she poked her head in the door window. Her mom had had an air mask on. Her little sister was lying lifeless on the table while the nurses took turns pressing her chest with their fingers. Debby was so frantic about the fact that they would not let her see her baby that she almost was unaware that she herself was gasping for breath.

She did not recall the rest of how it ended for her Mom. She did remember that for several months her Dad had been telling her how important the job of the older sibling was going to be.

Now he was saying how important it was that they had each other.

Doris turned and looked at Kathleen's face and saw that she is crying as much as her. She apologist for ruining what was supposed to be a fun day. Kathleen's response was that she had made it better

While the girls were shopping the guys had gone about the business of a lazy afternoon. James and Danny had gone to their tree house. Don and Allen were in the garage chit chatting about the joys of family life. Don had been telling Allen how jealous he was of him. Allen was trying to figure out why. Don looked up surprised at what he said then explained his side. He first told Allen to look around at everything he had. The farm the house the wife the family. All the things that they as kids had talked about having was now there in front of him. Allen had always talked about how hard it is to be the right kind of father. Don however, knew that they were great kids.

Don started to get in the driver's seat of Allen's Cadillac. Allen lowered his brow and shook his head and pointer finger at him. They walk out and glance over towards the tree house to watch the boys swing on the tire swing. Allen knew his brother was right he did have a lot. However, the older they got the more challenging it was. Kathleen had Allen stumped with the teen drama. One night she had come to his Door in the middle of the night because she could not sleep. Allen followed her back to her room and just sat there until she fell asleep. If she had been younger she would have asked for a story to be told. These days it is an everyday job for Allen to figure out what she needs. Allen had learned in the past few years that the things he used to do are slowly becoming non effective.

Allen had no regrets of years that had passed his daughter will always be his little girl, but faster than he would like she was becoming a young lady. James is getting older too, Doris and Allen recently agreed to let him get a job in town. Being a hard worker is one thing but he needed to see that he can do it some other place besides own his backyard. Danny seemed to have a little trouble finding his place sometimes. Allen could tell that he was a smart kid. There are those times however that he acts as though he can't tell you right from left. He could not tell if he doesn't want to push himself or if it just really comes in spurts like that.

Don had no personal experience in raising Kids but it seemed to him that Danny was overwhelmed.

The way Don saw it was that Danny was the youngest. His older sister loved him to death but she was not only smarter than him but is smarter than the average teenager. Then James who now had a job and is growing up too. Danny was always feeling one or two steps behind them. He might just feel like he should just stop trying.

Allen thought of the last couple days and how nice it

had been to just be brothers again. He was reminded of a time when they were kids and their Grandma Lane would come over. They both would watch out the window for her car and then run out almost knocking her over with their hugs. The best part of her visit was trying to guess what desert was going to come out of her cake pan.

Don loved the idea of being close to his brother. However, his life in Lubbock was waiting for him as well. The cotton farm was his home and there was a sense of security in his isolation. The main reason was if there was no one there, he could not offend anyone. Loneliness was however lonely. This was the reason Don spent so much time calling Allen in the last couple years. It was also the reason he had no trouble dropping everything to help find Danny. Don had a lot to think about. Allen had hinted several times in the last couple days that he could stay but he just thought he needed to get home at least to think it all through. His thoughts were interrupted by the truck pulling in. Don and Allen both ran out to unload the groceries for the girls.

THE DISCUSSION

Allen and Doris had talked among themselves several times. Don had not committed to staying with them but he was here now. When Allen called Don to come he knew that Don would not hesitate to help. When he got there and they saw the interaction don had with the boys Allen was willing to do anything to get Don to stay. Doris was not always sure how she felt but she did know that over the years she had grown to know Don pretty good because of his frequent calls to Allen. She had not spoken with Don all that much but Allen would always report in detail on every call. She knew that the bond that they had was somewhat similar to what she would've had if her sister had lived. The reality was if Don did stay things were going to change. Allen Knew that Don had hit on something with Danny they need to include Danny in more of his own adventures he was at the age where he could use an experience of his own without his older siblings hovering over him. Having an uncle around would help with that. Allen had managed to convince Don to take a family trip to the Lusters, because of the promise he had made to the Lusters. Allen had time until then to talk him into staying longer.

Allen and Doris thought they need to have a talk with James and Kathleen. Just to see how they were doing with all that was going on. Danny had given them all a scare and now that Don was there things were going to change. James was excited about Don being there he went on about how Don had been teaching him things about his radio and telling him about his airplane Don had promised to give him a ride someday. Kathleen was still not comfortable with Don. Her first question was when was he going to leaving. When then told her that they had asked him to stay longer she was not happy.

While they were talking inside Don had Danny were outside giving the Lusters motor home a bath. When Danny first went outside the question he asked was weather to start on top or on bottom. Don told him that starting from the top and working down was what he had in mind. Danny then bent down and looked at all the mud underneath and asked if they were going to clean there as well. Don nodded his head and said that it would get a bath too.

While Don was filling the bucket with soap and water Danny was staring intently as the suds started to form. Don then took the hose and spayed the camper down. Danny saw how much fun Don was having and asked if he could have a turn as well. Don paused for a moment and then showed him how to use the nozzle then stepped to the side as Danny pointed the sprayer. Don then told Danny that he was sure those tree branches overhead might have been a little dusty but he might try pointing the nozzle at the camper.

Danny moved the nozzle down pointed it striate on. As he got closer the pressure spayed back and splashed Don in the face. Don shook his head to get the excess water off him. Danny oblivious to what had just happen continued to spray. Don turned to get the bucket of soapy water. When he turned back around he saw Danny dumping the soap bottle on the back tire. Danny then said that he was going to start at the bottom and work up, because the top was too high for him to reach. Don told him that they could meet somewhere in the middle.

At this point Danny had not only poured most of the soap onto the tire. He was also now using the palm of his hand to smear it on the hubcap and work his way up the body of the camper. Don was trying to hide his grin but he gave up. He final just started to laugh out loud. He now was trying to decide if he was going to teach Danny how to wash the camper or enjoy the comedy show from it being done his way. There was no permanent damage being done thus it was worth it to allow Danny's inaccurate yet much more comical approach to prevail.

Inside the house Allen and Doris were still trying to unravel the mystery of Kathleen's dislike of her Uncle. She had said that the sooner He left the sooner they could get back to the way it was before. Both Doris and Allen tried to remind her that Don was the one that found her brother in the forest. Kathleen said that if he had not of shown up it would have been her that had gone with Allen to look for him. The other thing was Danny was there safe. They did not need Don here anymore. Allen and Doris look at each other and back Kathleen. James had disagreed with Kathleen few times over the years today however was one of those times. In return Kathleen gave him the same look that she always had. The thing that James liked the most about Don was how much Danny seemed to love him. He also though it was nice having another guy around.

They all glance out at the interaction between Danny and Don. Kathleen could not ignore the interaction between them. She still had some reluctance there was something about Don that still made her wonder what was going on.

Allen is looking out the window watching Danny use the hose as sword. He was apparently fighting the dragon that seems to be in front of the camper. Don walked in and Allen asked him how he manage the suds in his hair. Don told them about Danny's curiosity and how it was causing them to get as much as a bath as the camper. He recapped some of the afternoon and by the time he got to the soap on the tires the family was laughing so hard that they were in tears.

Don went back outside to finish washing and then cleaned up the mess. After they were done.

He climbed the steps of the motor home waved his hand to motion Danny to come as well, he then offered him some sweet tea. Danny saw the box that Lara had sent with only crumbs of choc chip left. After a moment of a well-rehearsed puppy dog face. Don had nodded his head and Danny was devouring the morsels that were left.

OFF TO THE LUSTERS

They had made a plan to try to arrive at the Luster's by twelve. Doris however had insisted on a large breakfast. Kathleen was not happy when she was awakened at ten o'clock. She tried tossing a pillow or two but Allen's persistence never had been a match for hers. He announced that it was time for breakfast and walked out of the room. Kathleen tried to pretend she did not hear him, but she knew her time was up. When she did finally make it to the table she was disappointed because to bacon was almost gone. She quickly grabbed a slice before doing anything else.

Doris believed that all road trips long or short should have snacks. Today she was not limited to the small space of their car. Therefore, she had been up since early morning preparing for the event. She was now busy wrapping the cookie platters and making the icing for the cinnamon rolls. She had also prepared several real meals for their two-day trip. They were sure that the Lusters would want to treat them to their food as well. Never the less the camper was being stocked with the loving touch of Doris Lane.

When they finally did, leave Allen sat in the front with Don. They talked about the memories of growing up in Lubbock. Doris and Kathleen sat at the table playing rummy. James watched out the window trying to spot any out of state license plates and Danny sat on the back bed pretending he had a steering wheel in his hand. Every time the motorhome moved the slightest in any direction he lean his entire body like it was a race track. Later on James was nice enough to show Danny how to play a game called fifty-two card pickup. Danny thought it was fun the first three times but soon got bored.

When they pulled in the driveway, all three of the Lusters were standing outside. Just as Don was reaching for the break, Addison caught his eye. His glance turned into a stare and Allen gave him a grin. Kathleen, James and Danny were the first to leave the motor home. Allen and Doris followed and then Don. As Don got out, he approached Quinn, Addison and Laura. He gave his greeting and began to introduce everyone. He started with Danny and worked his way up to Allen. Kathleen had given a dramatic curtsy, James tipped his cowboy hat, and Danny just waved.

It was not very long after this that Laura, Doris, Kathleen and Addison left to finish the meal. Laura had made ham hocks with beans, and jalapeno cornbread. When the guys walked in the door, they stopped for a moment turned and gave their attention to the pot cooking on the stove. They all gave a long sniff of their nose, and continue across the room. While the women finished lunch, they moved the room around so they could all fit the table.

When they gathered at table Laura was giving Doris cooking tips, Allen, Don and Quinn discussed logistics of how the motorhome was working out for them. Don then asked about the Field that he had landed in and Quinn assured him that compensation for the damage was not necessary. James and Danny did not say much but played a nonstop game of rock, paper scissors. By the time the meal was over Doris had a stack of new recipes to take home, Quinn had agreed to let Don do some work around the house and Danny was ahead by one on how many rounds he had played with James.

After lunch, the girls settled down to relax in the living room. Don, Allen, James and Danny went on the guided tour of the property outside. It did not long for James and Danny wanted to see Don's airplane. Don looks over at Allen the make sure it was ok. Allen waved his hand as to push them away. Therefore, Don took James and Danny to the barn where he had parked his plane.

After they left Allen turned to Quinn for some advice. He was not sure how to deal with Kathleen and her teenage drama. Quinn asked how old she was and whether she had a boyfriend. Allen answer Quinn gave Allen a look before he replied.

Quinn told Allen that there was no one answer for that question. He also said Kathleen was at the age for gaining responsibilities but she still needed guidance. He agreed that Allen was in new territory but also reminded him that she was too. The next thing he said was no matter how much he wanted to fix things, it was some times better to stand back and let them figure out what to do. Quinn then pointed out that the bravest thing could do is tell her that he did not have the answer.

Allen stopped for a minute to think about what he said and Danny came running over from the other side of the yard. Don had offered to take the boys up in his plane and he wanted to know if it was ok. Allen glanced at Don and James who are not far behind Danny. Don used his pointer finger to make a circular motion. Allen used his finger to give the same motion back. Don, Danny and James went back to the plane and Allen and Quinn went in to see what the women were doing. Quinn though he saw Laura mixing up cranberries before he left the house.

When they walk in the house, the first thing they noticed was the aroma of cranberries in the oven. Allen could already taste the bread just from the smell that was the room.

It was hard but he was able to keep his manners in check and he did not run to the kitchen, as he wanted to. When he got there however, the bread melted in his mouth.

As he thought about how good it was, he did not even realize that he had closed his eyes, to enjoy the flavor of the bread.

SOMETHING LIKE THAT

Don walked in the door with Danny and James trailing behind and asked Quinn if he could make a trip to electronics store. While he was in the airplane, he realized that the intercoms were not working. Quinn grabbed his hat and keys and headed out the door. Don had noticed that James was quite interested when they were flying, so he asked Quinn if there was room in the truck for him as well. Quinn said that there would be plenty of room and they could in fact just take the car instead. When they got outside Quinn opened the trunk to move a box of tools. Don took he box from him and Quinn told him that it could go anywhere in the trunk as long as he did not put it on top of the turkey roaster. Don hesitated for a moment because he thought Quinn's Dry humor was popping out. however, as he put the box of tools in the trunk he saw the turkey roasting pan in the far right corner. Don laughed as he returned to the front seat.

The electronics store was in the middle of town in between a general store and a Dairy Queen Don is sure that the side trip, of the unscheduled landing in Quinn's field was probably the one of the better parts of the trip. He had not completely sorted out how he felt about Addison, he knew that there was something there that he was sure was like nothing he had ever experienced before.

The reason he was staying at a distance was he although had a life in Texas and saw no need in perusing anything that would end when he left.

Quinn interrupted his thought with some question about what he found at Allen's, Don told him about his brother's farm and that Allen in a roundabout sort of way had asked him to move there. They then talked about the motorhome, Quinn told him not to worry about when he brought it back. Don also told Quinn about finding Danny and everything involved there. Don then told him that he needed to get back to Lubbock as soon as he could. Quinn offered to let Allen drive the motorhome back to his house. And the other details could be worked out in time. Quinn and Don continued to talk right up to the front door of the hardware store. Just before they walked in the door that last thing Quinn said was He had never seen his daughter's eyes sparkle quit so much as when she saw Don.

Don scanned the shelves for the parts he needed while Quinn and James wander around in the store. James had gone back and forward to the different isles. He passes a shelf with several different kinds of cables in various different lengths, the next shelf had extension cords in every size imaginable. Then there was an entire row of table top microphones. Just when he was starting to get bored his interest was hit again by the sound of the radio on the next shelf.

"C q, C q, C q this is whisky, Quebec, five, Bravo, calling C q."

James moved in closer but the radio was quite again so He started to walk away. He stopped when he heard a voice from behind him telling him not give up so easy. An older man walked up and James turned at the sound of his voice. Jack reached up to adjust the volume then he took the microphone.

"Wq5b this is November, five, bravo, mike, uniform"

Jack answered the interested look in James eye by making him more interested.

Quinn is now watching from behind as well. Jack explained to James that he was talking on what was called a Ham radio. James was a little confused he had worked on a farm all his life and ham came from a pig. Jack answers this by telling him that the name came from the word amateur, otherwise known as amateur radio operators.

"N5bmu this is wq5b Chuck in Midwest Texas"

James and Jack both turn as the radio came alive again. Don had found Quinn and started to announce himself but Quinn put his hand up then pointed in the direction of James. Don nodded and watched the interchange with the radio. Jack and James both talk on the radio for another few minutes. Jack had told Chuck that he was in a shop in Indiana. He then had told Chuck about James and let him talk as well. James did not say much more on the air other than his name and age. It was however quite obvious how excited he was. Quinn and Don, stood there laughing to themselves. At first they stood at a distance to let James have his fun, later they move closer when they realize that he was so involved, that their presents might not be noticed.

As James talked with the man on the other side of the microphone, Quinn and Don caught the eye of the store owner. Jack nodded at the interest James had of the radio.

When James was finished he turned his attention towards Jack again then asked Don if he could get a study book. Don did not have a chance to answer before Jack told him that he could have it free. James thanked him, Don and Quinn look at the title of the book and smile again.

On the ride home James could barely keep quiet about the fun he had with Jack and his radio or the fact that he was able to use it to talk all the way to Texas.

While they were gone Doris, Addison and Laura had been talking about Don. Allen and Kathleen were playing a game of rummy and Danny had move onto the front porch to play with his matchbox cars. When James came in the house he was just about to burst with excitement. He ran to Doris and Allen and told them about his fun. They had not seen him this excited about anything since the pinball machine was put into the seven eleven back home. Everyone in the room looked over at Don and Quinn. They both nod and point to James while he recapped the events of the afternoon with the enthusiasm of a Christmas morning gift exchange. His was so enthusiastic they could not help being excited just because he was.

He showed them the book that Jack had given him and tried to explain the code a guy named Morse had come up with. He further explained that it had been used all over the world by thousands of people. James held up a yellow worn out book titled **international Morse code**. The front cover had a picture of a Morse code keyer he pointed it out and asked if he could have one.

Don did not stay at the house long because he wanted to work on his plane. He asked his brother to help him,

Allen did not say anything but made eye contact with
Doris. He then got up from the chair and followed Don out
the door. Don knew that the problem with the intercoms
was a bad connection and stringing a new line under
the seats was going to be easier than trying to find the
problem with the existing line. Neither Don nor Allen say
much of anything for a while until Allen broke the silence.
He was on the opposite on the side of the plane from Don
crimping a new plug.

"What do you think of Addison."

Allen had seen how Don responded when he first saw
Addison, but he had also noticed that Don had been doing
his best to avoid her the entire time. Don looked up from
under the seat. He said nothing right away but spoke after
his head was down again.

"She's a cute girl"

Allen laughed and Don admitted that she was more
than cute. Don then pointed out that there was no use
pursuing his feelings any further because in another week
he would be gone. Allen's eyebrows went up and down
again and he just glared. Don answer his glare with his
own. Allen was trying to figure out what was drawing
Don to going back, and to Don it was obvious.

He had his job at the resort, the commitments to keep
as a mechanic, and most of all his chicken farm. Don also
pointed out that their father had taught them about how
to treat a lady. If he had found out that Don was making
advances at a girl that soon after he meet her he would
probably come down here and skin his hide just like when
they were kids.

They both climb down from the plane. Don had made

a strong case so Allen decided to drop it. Don did know there was a part of him that would love to see what is behind what he felt about Addison, but he needed to get home. His art of avoiding Addison had to indeed be a skill, and one more lost love in his life was more than he could bear. Don put his focus on the logistics of travel plans back to Allen's, and also his trip home. It was nice that Quinn had offered to store the plane, but the normal routine had to show his face some time and the longer he waited the harder it would be to go back home.

The disadvantage Don had was his brother was fairly good at talking him to just about anything. When Allen reminded Don that he had promised James a ride in the plane and so Allen drove the motor home back to his house and Don flew with James as his copilot. Doris and Laura had worked their magic in the kitchen and had transformed, flour sugar and chocolate chips into a soft chewy cookie. The cranberries, flour and butter became cranberry bread. An abundance of love was added to both as they were stashed in the motorhome for the trip home.

The time finally came for the Lane family to depart but within the time that they were there it seems that much had changed. The family bond between the Lusters and the Lanes seem to be automatic. Allen felt like Quinn had some good advice about parenting. It was nice to see James excited about something. Laura had given Doris and Kathleen some of her family recipes Danny was just happy that his brother got him a new set of hot wheels. Allen, Doris, Kathleen and Danny said goodbye and left with the motorhome. Don and James were left before they left Don had one last thing to ask Quinn.

THE FLIGHT TO CLOVERDALE

Don left James where the plane was to find Quinn and Laura for on last fair well. Their first question was when he thought he would be back their way. Don was hesitant to answer but finally said it would be a while. He was going home to his life in Texas. He had left in a hurry because of Danny but it was time to get back to his normal routine. Laura then left and Quinn said one last thing. It was obvious to Quinn the sparks that were flying between Don and Addison. It was also no secret that Don had been steering clear of her the whole time he was there. Quinn however wanted to make sure that Don knew how Addison felt. Don had spent so much time avoiding how he felt about her that he had no idea how he was making Addison feel in return. Don was reluctant but nods his head to acknowledge what Quinn had said.

About this time James walked up and is standing there waiting for Don. Quinn put his hand on Don's shoulder then pulls him into a hug. After this he turns to James. He was excited to be the copilot. He did not say anything but Quinn could see him bubbling inside almost to the point of spilling out his ears. James shook his hand and Quinn returns with a firm grip. Don and James made their way to the other side of the house where the plane is. On the way there James asked if he was supposed to do the preflight check himself.

Allen had driven many different vehicles over the years so the adjustment to the motorhome was minimal. Doris was at his side they had been talking about the events of the last couple days.

"A turkey roaster?" Doris questioned

Allen had told her about a conversation he had with Don. Quinn and Laura kept the roaster in the trunk of their car. They had said that as little as they use it there was no reason to leave it in the house. They also did not have a shelf in their cupboards big enough to hold it. In their mind it was the be the best place to keep it. Doris thought Maybe she could put theirs in the back of Allen's Cadillac. Allen hesitated for a minute then snapped his fingers. He reminded her that they did not have a turkey roaster. Doris then explained that now that she had a place to store one that. Allen stop her with the nod of his head. Doris grinned at Allen and changes the subject.

She thought it was nice of Don to offer to help the Lusters. She then asked Allen if he thought Don will come back. Allen really don't know he thought Don wanted to but he had too much pride to let go of his old ways. Allen said he might visit him at some point. Doris was ok with that but she wanted to make sure Allen did not forget about his family. She did not want him gone all the time. Doris turned and looked at him to make sure he knew she was serious, she needed him home. They had talked about Don staying so they could see more of each other. Don was gone now and she did not want Allen to go chasing after him to change his mind. Allen told Doris he thought Don just needs some time to think about it.

At first Danny did not know what to do without his big brother to torment him. Kathleen had quickly seen the need and engaged with him as the need arose. Doris glanced back every so often to check on them. It made her proud to see Kathleen take such a role with Danny.

Kathleen had kept Danny entertained the entire trip home. They played slapjack and hot wheels. They watching cars pass on the road they also talked about Uncle Don and his presents in their life.

Doris had been looking through the recipes that Laura given her. Allen had pointed out several that he wanted her to try. One was microwave rocky road another one Sausage cheese balls. As they got into town they stop at the local store and Danny jumped out and ran for the candy isle. Kathleen had followed him in and was making a selection of her own. The Seven-Eleven was a frequent stop for then it was close enough to home that they had ridden their bikes their numerous times.

Five minutes later as they rolled into the drive of their house Danny was chewing on his whoppers, Kathleen was slurping on a strawberry shake and both Allen and Doris were finishing their snickers candy bars. Allen stopped just beyond the gate to let the dogs out then continued to the house. Clyde and Pumpkin roamed the field expelling loose energy that they might have.

Dons estimated time frame was pretty close. Just about the time they got into the house Allen could hear the faint sound of the propeller over the field.

"Pilot to copilot do you copy"

"This is copilot, go ahead"

Don and James had been talking over the intercoms nonstop ever since they took off at Quinn's house and it was going to be an even chance between them of who like the radio better. James had seen this field a hundred times but this was a first to see it from this angle. James thought about how cool it was. Don knew that the road between the fields we kind of slim for a skyward approach but towards the back of Allen property had the width he needed to make his approach. The landing took about ten minutes and as the plane came to a stop Don jumped out of his seat while James just stayed there for a minute to take it all in. As James got to the ground his excitement caught up with him.

James ran off to express his enthusiasm to the rest of the family. He also knew that there was about a thousand and one snacks that were brought home he was sure there had to be something left for him. Don was back sitting in his seat he had taken on last look of the plane. His focus was that he wanted to get back to Lubbock before the end of the day. The weekend was coming which meant the resort would need a pilot for their tours

TIME TO THINK

There had been several times since the Lanes departed that Adison's pen hovered motionless as she attempted to express how she felt. She now walked the path that lead around her parents' house and she thought again of what words she could use to portray the rollercoaster that that she was on. Addison had been making plans to be away in South America two months but now she just did not know what to do. When she met Don she knew that there was more to him than just a handsome man. He however had spent so much time avoiding her that it was hard to tell if he had felt the same way. Still there was this hope that he would return.

Addison's journal had always been a way to express her process. She was however not completely sure what was going on, thus it was hard to put on a page. She was starting to wonder if her trip abroad was the best idea. What If Don did come back and she was gone.

The emotions that she felt were true and heartfelt. She knew that they were real because of how she felt about them. These were not emotions that could have been expressed merely by words on the page. Addison did come to a place where she able to process how she felt. When the words came all she can put on the page was

Love at first sight is not a myth and we shall see What becomes of Mr. Don Lane.

She closed notebook glanced at the clock then went to the front room where Laura was pulling an apple pie out of the oven. Addison started to grab a piece. Laura gave it a firm look and she sat in her chair. During most of lunch Addison stared into space and Laura and Quinn gave silent gestures in response. Quinn finally broke the silence by saying how empty the barn looked without the plane. Suddenly the bite of mac and cheese that was intended for Addison's mouth was on the floor. Addison pushed back to pick up the mess, Quinn and Laura look at each other and smiled.

They could see that Addison's mind was full and they encouraged her to her talk.

She told them about the commitments she had made to her church. She had helped them for the last year plan and raise money for a missionary trip but now she was feeling like she should not go. She thought it was crazy but she felt like she should drop everything to go after Don instead. When she stopped Laura said that she just needed to decide what was at stake. Addison then turned to Quinn. He had only known Don for a couple weeks but he said so far every promise that Don had made had been kept.

Quinn, Laura and Addison continued to talk about Don through lunch and apple pie.

Addison was encouraged to follow her heart rather than her mind. Quinn and Laura both agreed the mission group would understand whatever decision she made. It was not as crazy as it sounded to drop everything to follow her heart. Then Addison finally said out loud the thing that had been troubling her the entire time.

"What if the real reason he ran off so fast is that he just does not like me?"

Quinn told her that Don was far too smart for that and his gut feeling was that the opposite was true. Quinn thought that Don was trying to resolve his feelings about Addison and at the same time he was also intent on his life back in Texas.

Later that afternoon Quinn and Addison went to the church. Addison knew after all she had done in the last year to help plan the trip, that a face to face talk would be a better way to break the bad news. On the way there she opened up again. She was not sure how to explain how she felt other than to say she just knew he was the one. Quinn told her that he understood and t that was how it was when he met her mom, He just knew.

When Don left he started to consider the last week. The excitement of his brother's family had been nice but his life in Texas was waiting for him. He had passengers that need a ride, engines to be rebuilt and chickens to feed. The only thing his house in Texas did not have was a cute girl named Addison. When he first saw her run out of the house in her blue jeans and tee shirt a curls bouncing behind her. Well it took every ounce of willpower he had not to pull her into his arms right there. Don however had some firm beliefs about respecting women that had been passed on from his parents.

Even now as he thought of it he could hear his father's voice telling him wait for her to get close to you before he moved in. The fact that that he had been able to avoid her gave him some relief. He would argue that the reason he avoided her was because he was leaving soon but deep down he knew that he was staying away so he would not get hurt again.

Back in Indiana Addison was just walking in the electronics store looking for her Uncle Jack. He was not really Addison's Uncle but he was her dad's best friend and had lived a block away from them for her whole life. Over the course of time he became Uncle Jack. He had always been playing with electronics and when he was a teenager he deicide that he was not happy about the fact that the closest electronics store was two hours away, so he opened his own. She turned her head looking down the aisle and walked towards the front. Jack appeared from a small room behind the sales counter. His arms were open wide as he walked over to see her. She had come in because he called Quinn looking for James. Jack retrieved a manila envelope from behind the counter.

He handed her the package and asked if she or Don could give it to James. Addison peeked inside and said that she would try to get it to him and Don had left several days before.

After James had come by the other day Jack remembered an article that he had read. The article declared the elimination of Morse code from ham radio test. It was done in efforts to boost the involvement of younger potential hams.

Jack had thought that James might have some fun talking in code. But it will take some time to get good enough to carry on a conversation. He had seen so many people lose their way in Ham radio simply because they stumble over the code. With this he could decide how interested he really is in radios. And if he still is interested in code he can do that as well. Addison took the book from Jack and headed towards the door it was not long after that she was eating more of her mom's apple pie. She was still wondering who had the key to unlock the mysteries of Don Lane she giggled as she thought of how much fun would be to find out.

Addison was now thinking of her mom and dad. The last couple years the fields been getting harder and harder for Dad to take care of. He had progressively been more focused on things he could do from his chair. It might have been the underlining reason why she backed out of the missionary trip. The reason Quinn kept farming up is that he had not been able to admit his ever growing years were catching up to him. Addison was a country girl by heart she although could not take on her dad's work load alone. She broke into a large smile as the thought of Don. Crossed her mind again.

THE TRIP TO LUBBOCK

When Don reached the small town that was on the outskirts of Lubbock he sat up and adjusted himself in the seat. He then prepared himself for his descend to the back part of his field. In another ten minutes he had climbed out of his plane and had made the jog to his front porch.

The newspapers from the last week had been scattered across from one side of the porch to the other. Don stopped and nodded his head then walked the side of the house to retrieve his red wagon. He was eager to see what adventures Charlie Brown had gotten into while he was gone.

He starting some coffee, then made some cheesy grits and sat in his chair. Don laughed out loud as he watched Charlie Brown go flying feet first because Lucy had pulled the football out at the last second. He did not take much time looking at the rest of the papers, he did however pull the comics out of them for easy reading later. Don got when he heard the fait sound of wheels rolling on the gravel outside. He looked out the window to see a small car rolling in the driveway. When the car got to the porch Don was standing outside waiting to see who it was. After a few minutes the driver side door opened and a medium build middle age woman stepped out.

"Mr. Lane?"

Don nodded his head and she continued

"Are you Mr. Donald Lane?"

"Yes, Can I help you?"

She told Don that she was from the Texas department of health and human services and she had something of his. Before Don had a chance to form an opinion about what they had that might belong to him, a dark haired girl stepped out of the back seat. She was clinging tight to a cabbage patch kid in one arm and a small blanket in the other.

"Mr. Lane, I would you to meet your daughter."

Don did not say anything at first because his mind was on the events of seven years ago. He had girlfriend at the time She was a gal he met and the resort that he flew to every week. The resort had made a deal with Don that as part of the pay for flying their costumers they gave him a free meal each day. Kelsey was a waitress at their restaurant and from the moment she poured the first glass of tea Don was hooked. He wasted no time trying to get to know her more He took her to her favorite restaurant, after he worked up the nerve to ask her out.

The social worker introduced Leah Grace to Don. She then told him that her mom had always called her Grace and that is what she answered too now. Grace had a tight grip on the woman's side but ventured over to check Don out. As she slowly moved closer to Don she reached out her hand to touch him.

"Are you my daddy?" she finally said

Don had bent down so he was eye level with her and was somewhat shivering in an effort to hold the tears back. The resemblance between them was so precise that there was no doubt that he was her Dad. Don really did not notice it at first but when the social work saw them together in her mind there was no mistake. Don was a little taken by surprise to say the least. Don thought about the time line when Kelsey broke up with him together with how old Grace was it all made sense.

The social worker said that there would be some follow up appointments but based on the references she had received from the mother and what she had seen from Don so far she thought the paperwork could come later. Grace, clearly had already connected with Don and to take her back now would just be cruel her Dad would take care of her from now on.

There were several boxes in the trunk of the car that were retrieved. She knew it was going to be a last minute surprise for Don so she got some stuff together to make sure they had what they needed. The other thing she knew that they would need was time to get to know each other saying nothing more and then got in her car and drove away leaving Don and Leah Grace standing there alone.

The first thing Grace asked about was if Don had known her mom he said that he did. Grace just about exploded with excitement. It turned out that Grace had grown up living in the apartment just behind the resort that Don worked at. Kelsey had been careful not to bring her in the days he was going to be there. Dons flights were always Friday, Saturday and sometimes Sunday so it all started to come together in his mind. After they broke up he remembered that she was not on duty quite as much and now he knew why. The question now was why after seven years is this the time for Leah to come along. As he thought of all this and how he was going deal with this change, one thing came to mind.

When they got inside Don gave Leah a glass of milk he was exploring the parcels that came with her. The boxes were full of everything from juice drinks, gummy bears and crackers to wet wipes to more toy dolls to extra blankets. There were crayons, writing paper drawing paper construction paper and paper towels too everything you could imagine for a seven-year-old, there was even a sleeping bag and pillow.

Don pulled the Barbie sleeping bag out and Leah discarded the cabbage patch kid and was reaching for the pillow that had fallen out of the bundle. It was a small one, sized for a little girl. White, well it looked like it used to be white. it was really kind of grey the way Leah held onto it seemed to Don it had brought her though a lot of tough times.

While Leah was playing with Dons matchbox car collection Don was on the phone with Allen.

Allen asked about Kelsey but that was one thing that Don did not know yet. The only thing he could tell Allen was a social worker had dropped Leah off and gave no info on Kelsey other to say she had given him good references.

Allen said that he thought Don was ready for anything now. Don thought about it and realized that he had to get some grocery's if he was going to be ready for anything all he had in house is eggs and grits. Don had learned a few things from his mom but he did not do much more than pot roast and omelets Allen hinted that he knew a place where home cooked meals are every day. Don had thought of that too but he had to get everything settled there with the social service and all. When he figured out what all is going on there he would then make plans.

Don hung up the phone and turned his attention to Leah. Don told her that they were needing some food and asked her what kind of cereal to buy. Without hesitation she said fruit loops was the best. Don nodded as he added it to list he had started on the pad. He then told her he was thinking they would go out for dinner and asked her if she like burgers. Leah had not said much but Don was surprised at how easy she had gotten over the insecure feeling that she had when she first got out of the car. Don then told her about his air plane and asked her if she wanted a ride. Leah's eye brightens again and she nodded her head.

Don's first stop was Safeway to get some milk and cereal. After they got there however Leah was nice enough to let Don know that there were a few other things they were low on as well. her list included blow pops, gummy bears and ice cream bars. Don gave in to most of her request as well the things he needed too including a step stool for Leah. As he looked over the things that Leah had chosen he decided that there was room in his wallet for one more stop.

"Ok Leah you can open your eyes now"

Her hands came down and her eyes popped open in one swift move. At first she just stared she turned to look at Don then turned back to look out the windshield. Don looked over at Leah

And said they could stay out in the car and stare or

they could go see what's inside. They crossed the parking lot and reached the door they were welcomed by a woman in a red vest.

Her greeting was the same thing she said to everyone that came in, welcome to Toys R us.

They stayed in the store for a good hour looking though all the toys and discussing which ones Leah had seen before and the ones that were new to her. It did not seem to Don that she was deprived of much of anything like he would expect to see from a girl in foster care. There also was not doubt in his mind she was a Lane. Her brown hair, blown eyes, her face looked just like his dad and the dead giveaway was how much she nodded her head as a response she was a Lane for sure.

Don told Leah that she could have something for a welcome home gift. When they got to the checkout isle he just laughed at the decision she finally made. It seems as though when he first saw her several hours ago he thought she was all about the dolls the extra dolls in the box seem to point that direction as well. But the evidence that he was facing now seemed to point to a different direction all together.

She had looked on every side of the box by now and had asked three times if she could open it in the car. Don told her to wait until they got home he didn't want her to lose any of the pieces.

After they got home the first order of business was testing out the new step stool while they worked together to put the groceries away. After Leah had done her part it was to the couch opening her new toy. She had chosen a hot wheel's race track so she could use the matchbox cars that she had been playing with before they left.

After Don got it set up for her he watched from the kitchen. It did not take long to realize that the next job would be cleaning out the frig and pantry. A task that would have to be done more than once a year which was his current track record. After twenty or thirty minutes he finally got all the groceries put in their place. He had picked up a kids cook book at the toy story and as he turned the corner to look at it with Grace he realized she was sound asleep on the couch with about five of his hot wheel's cars on top of her.

His previous plan of burgers was replaced by Domino's pizza for the simple reason that they delivered. Don was temped pick up where he had left off with Charlie Brown. He knew however that the stack of papers that came with Grace were not going to read themselves so he started to look through them. The dates on the documents confirmed his theory about when and how grace came along. As Don started to read though the papers he was confronted with the reason Grace had come.

The first thing he saw was a letter from Kelsey stating the instructions on who to contact should anything happen to her. Mr. Donald Lane and his current address. It not only said that he did not know about Grace, but it was also very clearly stated that there was no other option than to give Don full parental rights no questions asked. This was probably the references that the social worker was referring to.

Then Don found a newspaper article from the Buffalo springs. As he read it he started to cry. The story in the paper told about a fire that had started in the back room just behind the main building of the resort. The suppression system keeps it from spreading to the dining room of the resort, however the small apartment that had been added the back part of the building was burnt to the ground. The quote that made him cry was an eye witness account of someone seeing Grace crawl through the window just before the walls came crashing down. As Don read the paper he could just imagine Kelsey refusing to think of how much danger she was in until her Daughter was safe. After he read that he decided that was enough for night. Grace was already asleep on the couch so he would use his recliner and he would be there for her when she woke in morning, or perhaps if she was up in the night.

After Allen hung up the phone he knew that Don needed him now. He decided that he was going to go to Lubbock soon. Allen told Doris that Don had not said he was coming back, but when it was suggested that Allen knew a place that had home cooked meals and free rent he did agree. Doris decided that it was close enough for her. She was going to get her dad moved into the guest room and they would work out the other details latter. Allen bought a ticket to Lubbock. Allen could of drove to Texas but he was pretty sure Don was wanting to Bring Leah to Indiana in his plane it was just a matter of how long it would take. Allen was pretty sure Don would want him to come with him.

ALLEN IS THERE

The next morning as Grace crawled out from under the sleeping bag she looked over to see Don stirring a pot on the stove. The cars fall off her belly as she gets up and Don turned at the sound. He held up the pot and offered her some grits. Grace nodded with her sleepy eyes and walked over and sat at the kitchen table. Don met her there with a glass of orange juice and a bowl of fruit loops with a dab of grits.

Don realized the night before was his old way of life had been changed dramatically. He never did like change. Allen was on his way he would help to iron out the details of what would take place in the months to come.

Don had been up early going over the documents concerning Leah Grace. His focus this morning was would social services be ok with a move to Indiana. Don looked through the laws concerning child adoption it seems that it would be ok. On the other hand, it was really not an adoption. Grace was his Daughter not only could you tell just by looking, but there was also the letter from Kelsey assuring him full parental rights no questions asked. All that being said he did have to wait for the follow up from social services to make his move. The only problem was the women who brought Grace left no indication of when that would be. Today, tomorrow, next week, next month.

He just had to wait. The upside to waiting was there was more time to make plans and put things in place to ensure that Grace is cared for in the best possible way.

Don sat down next to Grace and asked her if she like being called Leah or Grace. She said Grace was fine it reminded her of her mom. Then she chomped some fruit loops down.

Don asked Grace what she wanted to decorate her room with. She said space would be cool but she liked anything as long as it was not Barbie. Then she said that she also would really love her room to look like the ship from Goonies. Then she said that the most important thing was to make sure there was room for her pillow. Don felt proud of himself he was getting to know Grace and also having a fun project planning time as well. Don told her that she could have her room in whatever design she wanted. He also told her that he had planned on taking her to Meet her Uncle and his family in Indiana. He would want to stay there for some time so she could get to know everyone. The loss of Grace's mom will always be there but her eyes lit up more every time she heard about another member of the family that she did not know she had.

After breakfast Don and Grace went out to the barn to collect eggs. He had six chickens all of them he named after the peanuts cartoons carters. He named Lucy because she always seems to be bossing one of the other chicks around, that one was Charlie Brown. Pig pin was because another one that seemed to always be in the mud. The other three were named at random but it only seemed right to have Linus, Snoopy, Woodstock in there as well. As they walked to the area where his airplane was they passed a barn where the goats, cows and horses once lived. Don thought of the promise he had made to his Dad and all the things that had come up since then to prevent him from keeping it up like he wanted to. When they got to where the plane was Grace was still focused on the chicken that had followed her out of the shed. Lucy had been pecking at her feet ever since they left.

Don walked over and opened the side door then tipped his just like he would do for one of the passengers on their way to the resort. Don then took her by the hand and walked her up the step ladder. He buckled her in and sat in the seat next to her. He started the engine and a few minutes later the plane stared to move slowly ahead. The excitement that Grace, came in several stages. At one point she had stiffened up and was griping the side if the seat with all her might. She loosened her grip as the speed began to build. Just when Grace thought she had been handling all the excitement, the front wheels began to lift. Don glanced over and he recalled how he felt on his fist couple times. He then did a silent laugh nodded his head and turn back to the controls.

Don asked her if she had ever been in an airplane before. She did not say anything but shook her head then gripped the seat again. Don turned the plane and lowered the altitude. He then told her to look out the window and she would see where they lived. Grace glanced out to see the house and the surrounding land of Don's farm after this her tense mood started to lighten. She laughed when she saw Don's last name that had been painted in big letters on the roof of the house. There was also a larger than life yellow hand next to it.

He didn't say anything but turned and nodded as the plane made a turn he then headed to the airport to pick up Allen. Grace had a similar response to the landing than she did to the take off. When they approached the place where Allen and Don had agreed to meet Don was trying to decide if he was going to tell Grace that his brother was a twin. He then decided that he would just let things unfold as they would.

Grace looked and Don then Allen then Don again it was lucky for Grace that they had worn different clothes otherwise she would have been really confused. She made several commits about there being two of them. She however was soon listening to her Walkman in the back seat. While Allen sat in the front with Don. Allen asked how she was adjusting. Don said that he thought they were go through this whole weirdness time of her getting used to each other but instead of that time lasting couple days it ended up being couple hours. Allen committed on the family resemblance she had. Don thought that looking alike helped but she also seemed like she adjusted pretty easy to whatever she is into.

When Allen came he expected to find an insecure girl but he found a normal seven-year-old instead. Allen turned and looked at Grace who was shaking her head to the beat of whatever was on the other side of her headphones. Don said nothing, his focus was now on the landing of the plane in his field. After they landed Grace jumped out of the plane she looked to Don for his approval ran to the chicken pin.

Don and Allen gone to the house. Allen wanted to look over the stack of paperwork that came with Grace. He read the letter from Kelsey then he looked at the article about the fire that killed her. He saw a note stating that if Don had failed to take responsibility for Leah or if he displayed any behavior showing he was not eligible to care for her she would be put in foster care.

Allen then held up a one-page document stating that Graces name had been legally changed to Lane in the event of Kelsey's passing, per the instructions from her.

Allen spent an hour going through the different documents stopping from time to time to ask Don if he had seen this part or another. Each time Don replied that he had seen it all.

Don told Allen that Kelsey was always a good at planning for the unexpected. The thing he regret the most was he had always told himself that he would get back in touch with her but he had always found a reason not to go and find her. Grace just reminded Don of all the good times they had.

Allen put the folder away they both look out the window where Leah Grace was chasing the six Chickens. They both went out to the front yard to join the fun. Later on Allen had made burger the patties and the outside grill had been warmed up. Don brought out the barbeque chips and Allen told him not to put them on his shoulder. Don was going to throw one back his way but he was too busy with a Styrofoam airplane. Allen and Don both took turns with the dry humor. This time Don let him win. While Allen cooked dinner Don and Grace were having fun both with the Chickens and the toy plane. As Allen looked over at the interaction Between Leah Grace and Don, he recalled the way he responded when he saw Don with his kids at home. And he started to wonder if Kathleen would be able to see it as well.

Quinn was leaning over his model plane with a propeller in one hand and the tube of glue in the other just as a dab of glue was applied to the nose of the plane, the telephone came alive.

"dag nab it" Quinn blurted out

Not only did he miss the nose of the plane but the propeller now had to be unglue the form the table it was stuck too. He climbed out of his seat and reached for the handset for the phone. Quinn smiled when he heard Doris voice. She asked for Laura first then told him about Leah Grace. She also told him that Allen had gone there to help him and that Don might be heading back this way some time soon. When she was done Quinn hung up the phone shook his head then laughed out loud again. He searched the table by the phone for the slip of paper that Don jotted his number down on. He Picked it up then after a second later put the receiver back down and the paper back it back in its place

After Doris got off the phone with Quinn she sat in the chair to relax. They had spent the last three hours trying to get Grandpa George moved to their house. the first thing they had dealt with was he was not going to go without his favorite chair. Then the table next to had to come as well. Kathleen had been sent back several times for his medicine bag then his sweeter and his tea glass which was a fifty oz. mug that was always filled with ice tea. George only agreed to move into the house was on the premise that he was going to be helping Doris with the kids, he was never too much on admitting he needed help. Doris did not care He was in the house with them and the house in the back yard would be there for Don and Grace should they decide to come.

Doris told George that when he got settled in his chair that his task was going to be as simple as another pair of eyes on the kids. Doris would never tell him this but the biggest reason he was there was she need Kathleen at the house and sending her back to her dad's house every day was not something she could afford right now

NOW ON FROM HERE

Quinn had seen the faraway look in Addison's eyes several times in the last month. He was sure that she was going to need a place to let her feelings out. He tilted his head and gave her a look that had been rehearsed many times before. He caught her eye as she was dazing away.

She looked back at him does not say anything but left the table and they went out the door together. As they were leaving Laura walked in and Quinn told her they were going for a walk and would be back soon. Laura had seen the look in her daughter's eye as well, and knew that a walk with her Dad would be the best thing for her now.

By the time they got to the porch Quinn had already asked Addison what she had thought of Mr. Lane. In her attempt to avoid the question she asked which one. The reason Addison was avoiding the question was because she still did not know exactly how she felt. They had walked out to the dirt walkway. Quinn told her that Don had dropped everything to go to help find his nephew. Quinn also said that he had been willing to stay another week to make up for the damage he had done.

Addison's face seemed to soften even more. She still wondered about the fact that Don never had acted like he even saw her. He had spent most of his time in Addison's mind avoiding her all together. Quinn assured her that

Don had noticed her. He then said that Don had been avoiding her but for an entirely different reason than she than she had thought. Don was just too scared to admit he was attracted to her.

Addison asked him how he knew Don was attracted to her. He said the same way he knew she was attracted to him. Her face then turned red and she turned away and broke a smile. He said that was the easy part when he saw the way Don looked at her, he knew. It's also the first thing most guys do when they don't know how to handle something they avoid it. It was pretty clear to Quinn that Don was trying to figure out how he felt about Addison Just as much as Adison was trying to figure out how she felt about Don

Quinn had been around long enough to know that the main reason one worries about how they feel about another person is because they are wondering how the one they feel so strongly about, feels about them. It had to of been hard for Don. When he started out he was just going to help his brother. He had to make an unexpected stop just to get to where he was going and he also had to figure out how to get there without his plane. It was one of the things that made Quinn believe that he was such a good person despite the detours that came his way he found out how to make it all work. Don had completed his task and was on his way home back to the life he knew and then he met Addison.

Quinn had been tracking Addison's every move for over thirty years now and he knew how to reading between the lines. It was just a question of whether she was willing to admit that what he was saying was true.

She started by admitting that Don was cute and Quinn gave her a side glance. After that she admitted that she did like him but she did not know what to do. She had seen a lot of cute guys before but this one is different and now he was gone back to his life in Texas.

Quinn told her just to see what would have happened and that they were not in charge of when the right one came along. If Don was Mr. right she was not going to make him stay away.

He hesitated but then decided to let the secret out.

"I think he is going to make a great Dad too."

Addison turned and gave him a look of disbelief trying to decide if she had heard him right. He answered her by saying he was not talking about her and that Don already was a father. She again was hit with disbelief but this time it was mixed with anger and mistrust. Quinn then told her the rest of the story and her mind was at ease again.

They were back on the front porch now and Quinn asked her if she was worried about getting the two bothers mixed up. He would have not liked to see her give a loving Gaze to the wrong Brother. She was confident that despite how much they looked alike that they were not the same. They walk in the house and are greeted by Laura's pan of fresh baked cookies. Addison took one and thought to herself that they were not the same at all.

After Addison went home Quinn and Laura sat in the living room they had been talking about the chain of events starting after Don landed in their field. He was not only thought to be the son they never had but the whole family was theirs as well. Then there was the obvious connection that Addison felt toward Don and the news of Leah Grace. They talked more about the Lanes and how much their life had changed rather than how it affected them. They finally decided to call the Lanes and offer their condo on New Mexico so they would have the option of a place to getaway if they should want to as a family. When they called Doris she told them that they would love it and they would let them know when they were going down.

Kathleen shook the arm of George to wake him up for Dinner he caught the scent of grilled cheese coming off the stove and she handed him a plate. Kathleen had been wondering a lot about Don. When she heard about Leah Grace the first thing that came to her was the idea of another little one to look after. She also had to admit that perhaps her judgement of him had been misplaced. She had been having Several heart to heart talks with her mom about how she felt. She had stood her ground but she could not deny that both of her brothers loved him. There also seemed to now be an explanation of what she was picking up on when he was there.

There was nothing about the atmosphere that Don did not like. It was just he did not know how to fit it to family that his brother already had. Kathleen's heart seemed to be in the right place and she was picking up on something but she had misjudged what the problem was. The other thing was she did not want to share her brothers and she was afraid that she was going to be replaced. Her role as big sister had been threatened by uncle Don. Doris had told her that she did not see that happen. She also said that it was a good thing when Don was there. James and Danny need another man in their lives. They are also getting older and can only take so much of big sister bossing then around.

Doris then reminded Kathleen of when she started shopping with her mom. There were so many things that they could not talk about unless they were away from the boys. How many times had she heard Kathleen say that the guys just don't understand? The thing that Doris was trying to tell her was guys need time away as well. Kathleen had looked at her with disbelief and asked what could guys have to talk about.

Just then the sound of James and Danny on the porch made Kathleen's face turn red wondering if they heard any of what she said. To her relief all they were worried about was the cheese sandwich as well as the kielbasa that was on the stove. Kathleen glanced at Doris and Doris returned with look of relief as well. Doris then said that things were going to be different if Don was to come again but it will however be a change for the better.

Meanwhile in Lubbock Don and Allen took turns telling stories to Grace while they ate their burgers. The first one started as a question from Grace about the amount of stuffed animal peanuts craters in her room. Apparently Don liked Charlie brown as a kid as well as much as he does as an adult, he had collected a stuffed animal of every one of the peanuts gang including pig pin.

Allen told her the story of having to stand behind the dog house while Don pretended to fly his plane. Grace started to laugh and put her hands out to pretended to fly her own plane. Don have always found that Charlie brown is a good way to laugh at life. Pour Charlie Brown never did get to kick that football.

While they were talking they heard a faint sound of a car in the distance. Don recognized the car that had rolled in the drive a week before. As The social worker pulled up Don and Allen stood to meet her in the driveway. She seemed a little stunned and thought she had been seeing double. She stepped out of her car Don was there. He greeted her then introduced his brother. Then told her that he had flown in from Indiana to help him get settled. She then turned to Grace and asked how she was doing.

Grace told her that she had a super cool dad. She told her all about his chickens, race cars and the grits every morning. She had gotten him mixed up with her uncle several times but it had turned out all right. She talked about her uncle and his farm in Indiana and her dads plane too. Grace then starts to pull her arm toward the back lawn. The woman told Grace that she could not stay long enough to ride in the plane and that she would see it another time.

The social worker motioned to her briefcase and they made their way into the house. It turned out that the final papers had already been done the woman had a gut feeling Don was going to be the best thing for Grace. Don and Allen then explained their plan about moving to Indiana to be with the rest of the family. She saw no problem with the idea. She said that it was actually a great idea the more family interaction she had the better off she would be. She then said that Doris sounded like a great woman and Grace would no doubt be well cared for. After a few more minutes She was gone again.

Don went out to show her off while Allen called Doris to check in. when Don came back in Allen told him that Doris had spread the word to Quinn and Laura. Don did not say much but his thoughts had automatically gone to Addison. He realized after he had left that he regretted trying to avoid her. Grace had just come in from her bedroom she had been playing with her cars and was dressed for bed. She came and sat down on the couch while holding on to the snoopy doll from her room. Don had just about decided that he was going to be in Indiana for a while. He need to ship their belongs to Indiana and perhaps after they are settled they could return with a truck if in fact he does decide to live there full time. The next morning all three of then loaded in Dons plane for the flight to Allen's.

Despite Addison's seat was in the back Don assured her that her help would be needed to get his plane in the air he told her that when she felt the front wheels come off the ground she should put her arms up and then pull back. He put his arm up and in front of him as if he was holding the stick of the airplane. Don continued to interact with Leah as they took off towards Indiana. As Allen Watched the interaction between Don and his girl, he cracked a smile at the thought of what parenthood had done to Don. Once they were in the air Leah's headphones went in and her attention was on the music it was mixed tape her mom had made. It had Alabama, beach boys and the beetles. Grace did not always like the choice of music, but because it was from her mom she had learned to love them all.

A PIECE OFFERING

Don was in Allen's living room scanning the shelve next to the wall. Allen walked in and asked him what he was looking for. Don turned and his face brightened with relief at the sound of his voice. Don said that he had been looking for a phone book for Shadeland. Allen knew that Shadeland was the town the Lusters lived and went to the kitchen drawer to retrieve the book that Don wanted. He then started to tease Don and asked if he had forgotten Addison's number. Don laughed as well and said that he wanted to send a pie to Addison. He was looking for the number for a bakery in the town close to their house. Don remembered that when he was there he had seen a sign on the window that said they delivered.

Don found the number for Aunt Millie's, bakery and the text of the ad that confirmed that they would deliver within a thirty miles of their store. Don did not know that Adison had canceled her trip and he thought she would be leaving the next day. He wanted to give her something before she left. Grace had come in and Don asked her what kind of pie she liked. She stopped to think for a minute a gave her answer to him. Don called the shop and the women on the phone identified herself as Millie. When Don told her what he wanted she said that she could have it done that afternoon. Don replaced the receiver then paused for a moment nodded and looked at Grace. He told her that her choose of pie was a berry good idea.

Grace went over and sat next to George and soon found herself in his lap. There was what some would call a contagious laugh with the interaction between them. It was fun for everyone to watch. George had always been good with the kids and Grace was soaking up every bit of love that he was giving her. She told him all about her Dads airplane and how fun it was to ride with him. She them told him about the larger than life hand that had been panted on his roof.

George reached in his pocket and pulled out a peppermint candy and gave it to her. He told her some of the things that Doris had done when she was her age. Her mom had been teaching her to cook and sew and he was the one who taught her to ride a bike and change the tires.

George then told her about some of the neat things she would be getting into while she was there. Some being the riding on the tractor, jumping in the leaves and the camper that her dad had. Grace turned to look at Don with an expecting look and Don Nodded at her in return.

She then jumped off George's lap and ran to Don and they went out to look at the camper. As they walk outside Kathleen and James follow. Allen and Doris Took the opportunity to relax in the living room and George faded off to sleep.

After they left Allen decided to take a snooze as well and Doris sat at the table with a deck of cards. Just as she was laying out a solitaire game Danny came in from outside. At first he stood there and watched her put the cards on the table. It was confusing a first while he was trying to guess why some of them were face down and others were up. Eventually, he asks Doris if she could show him how to play. She stopped for a moment then responded to him. She would teach him but she was going to have get a new deck of cards the one she had was missing a few cards. She made her way back to her room to get the cards and Danny sat down to match up the by color, all the black on one side and the red on the other.

When Doris came back in the kitchen, her eyes widen and she screamed as she saw the fire on the stove. Allen and George both woke when she screamed. Allen jumped up, to put the fire out. When they heard the scream from outside they looked to see the smoke from the kitchen window, Don grabbed the extinguisher from the back of the motorhome and went into the house by the time he got their Allen had out with the sink water. Then he went to Doris who is off to the side in tears. It was several minutes before she said anything and when she did all she could say was that she froze and it was all she could do to yell to Danny for help.

Allen and Doris are still hugging one another. Doris had turn on the oil to cook lunch and the second she was gone was when it got out of control. The flame never actually left the pan. Allen is very sympathetic of Doris and how scared she must have been. Don had gone outside again and told the kids what had happen. He then showed Danny where his living and bedroom was now that he was staying where George had been before. When they came back to the yard Allen was there and He asked about Doris. Doris was just scared and also a little mad at herself. Allen told her that he had been there too and he was just of much to blame as she was.

Allen turns his gaze to Danny and told him to pay more attention. He could have yelled for help before his mom got there.

Just about then James and Kathleen came back from the cleaning job at the back house when they heard about Danny's fireworks they went in to help Doris with lunch. Grandpa had been there in the house for the last week but Doris wanted it to be clean for Don and Grace.

Kathleen had bonded quickly with Grace and had started saying that she was her favorite cousin.

Don watched the interaction between Kathleen and Leah as James and Danny joined them as well. Don thought of Addison and was sorry he did not get to know her while he had the chance. He did not know what he was going to do now that Grace was with him. He thought that maybe when Addison returned from her journey below their paths would someday cross again.

Later that day Doris and Grace were in the kitchen. Doris is hold out a wooden spoon with choc chip cookie dough, it was in the shape of a cookie but not quite cooked. Grace licked he lips as she tastes the dough. Doris said it was almost done as she put the pan back in the oven.

She then turned to the counter beside her to the ones that came out only a few minutes ago so they were still warm but she thought Grace would like them. Grace crinkled he face at the site of the round odd colored appetizer but changed her toon as it went in her mouth. Grace nodded as she worked on the last few bites.

Doris told he that her dad like them too and it was

one of the recipes Laura had given her couple weeks ago. Grace then asked who Laura was Doris explain who she was and told her about the last time Don came and the storm that made him land in their field. Doris put a sheet of wax paper in each of the small boxes that she was using to pack the cookies in. Danny is there now hovering over the kitchen waiting for any stray cookies that might get loose. Doris handed him a peanut butter, a chocolate chip and a cathedral window cookie as she scoops each of them in their boxes. As soon as the last box is, done six total James, Kathleen and Doris make their way out to the camper to be stored for the weekend trip.

Addison is sitting in the front seat of the pickup truck waiting for Quinn. She had already seen the leader of the youth group to break the news to her about her change in travel plans but she wanted to be able to say goodbye to everyone. She felt kind of bad for dropping it in the leader's lap she had not only helped plan the trip but was, until last week she was going to be helping watch the younger kids of the group and had made several promises to them as well. The youth leader was understanding and stated that she had been in love once as well. Quinn jumped in the truck and started the engine almost simultaneously, after he put it in gear he pulled away before he says a word. Addison looks at him with a frustrated stare. Quinn assured her that they still had time it only took ten minutes to get there.

Addison wanted to have time to see everyone and say good bye some of them did not even know that she was not going. She wanted to tell them herself. On the way there Addison went through several highs and lows about the decision not to go but decided in the end that it was the best thing for her. If she was to find out that things were not going to work out here there would be other opportunity's down the road. When they pulled in the lot she was met by all her friends and the younger kids. Quinn slowed even more then finally stopped in the middle of the parking lot and Addison got out to greet her friends.

By the time Quinn made it over to the group Addison was in the middle of ten kids trying to get her attention. There was a loud moan in unison when Adison broke the news to her friends and another five minutes of hugging before she could break away. Her mind was made up that was for sure but the longer she stayed the harder it would be to leave; she did end up staying long enough to help the kids get buckled in for the ride to the airport. After this she ran back to the car where Quinn was waiting

When she got back in the car she asked if he thought that Don could be the one. Quinn looks over to her then looked back at the road as he smiles. Quinn said that was a question that only she could answer. He did tell her one way to find out. He told her to ask herself two questions. How did you feel when he left? How would you feel if he came back? Quinn drove into the drive way they both look up in surprise at what they saw. Mille was there in the house talking to Laura.

The nice thing about a small town was everyone was known be everyone else. Mille could be there swapping recipes with Laura or getting donations for the next bake sale and there was the alternative of just stopping in to say hi. All was reviled once they walked in. they were greeted with the smell of an elderberry pie Elderberry was the absolute all-time favorite desert for Addison and knowing this when Don asked for berry Mille knew that there was none other than would do. When she read the card she was surprised to see that it was from Don.

She read the card to herself she laughed under her breath it said I just wanted to let you know you both took and left a piece in my heart, enjoy your missionary trip.

The smile that cracked on Addison's face was just as big as Don's for Adison did not know Don was in Indiana. Quinn had convinced Laura that the unveiling of Don's current ware bouts would be better off revealed at a later date. Although They could not help but smile at each other when they saw the note.

Addison saw the look as she walked away but paid little attention. The focus was now on Don Lane and elderberry pie as she walked she held it up to her nose, after she was sure no one could see her she took a bite, prior to reaching the area of the kitchen where the utensils were. After wiping the elderberries off her nose she cut out the remainder size piece out of the pie tin

READOSSA

When Allen, Doris and Don woke up they loaded in the motor home. They had packed the night before so they were ready to leave early. They also had the kids camp in the motorhome so they could sleep on the way should Don or Allen decide to leave earlier than they planned. The kids also had asked because It looked like it would be a fun place to camp out. Doris had waving her wand over the stove and not only had she made lunch for everyone but she had also preparing her usual menu of road trip snacks. They were on the road and it was still several hours before they were ready to wake the kids.

Doris was still tired herself so she slept on the road as well. Allen drove and Don sat beside him. It was silent for several hours with little more than the input from Don about what was on the map. When Doris did wake up she did just as she would have had she been at home she stared to make her way to the kids to get them up. She then put the premade breakfast burritos in the microwave and started a game of solitary. When she sat down Danny came to the table and sat across from her. Doris started to lay out the deck but got up several times as the microwave called her name.

Don was now in the driver and Grace was on the floor in between Allen and him. All three of them had been in a consistent dialog since she woke up. Allen and Don had been telling Grace about their parents and the life they had growing up, Grace had been telling them about growing up with her mom. As time went on Grace laughed about the stories being told and when she did everyone seemed to laugh as well, just because the youngest laughers are always contagious. Later Grace sat with Danny at the table but they both ended up on the floor racing the hot wheels down the aisle. James had spent the day watching for truckers to get them to honk their big horns he would talk to a few on his Hand held C B.

Kathleen did number of things to occupy her time. She started out trying to paint Grace's nails. She had yelled from the back several times as the motorhome change direction asking to keep it striate. When she realized that the nail painting was not going to work they tried slap jack on the back bed and when Grace moved on to the cars Kathleen got out her word search book. It was late when they got in and Grace and Danny had already fallen asleep so Don and Allen carried them in.

The next morning while most of the family is sleeping in, Don was out for a jog. He saw a waterfall and he slowed a moment to take it in. As he started to look around he spent a minute or two just staring and contemplating the idea of falling in love. His thoughts were interrupted by a bump on his shoulder. Don looked over to see a young man in his early twenty's. He held a video camera and it was aimed at the falls. He did not see Don at first because he was looking through the viewfinder while narrating the scene in front of him. The camera was dropped to his side when he saw Don.

The boy was apologetic and seemed to be a little embarrassed. Don tried to ease his mind by starting a conversation with him. He then he introduced himself and asked if he had ever been there before. The boy said that had not been there before and he come up to stay the weekend for a family reunion. Don said he was there for a similar reason as well and told him about his visit with Allen's Family and the need to get away. Chad introduced himself and said that he had meet his Dad only two months ago and they had come out there to have some fun on the slopes.

At Chad's request Don took the camera and taped him narrating more of the scenery beyond the falls. As they got close to the lodge where Don was staying they could smell the faint scent of country gravy and Don knew that Doris was working her magic in the kitchen once again. When he went in he told Allen and Doris about his jog. Then he ate some crispy bacon while waiting for the eggs and grits. It was clear to Don that Chad had a look on his face that said his process had just begun. All three of them could not imagine growing up without a dad. It did however make Doris think about her mom.

Just then Grace came in with her favorite pillow and her snoopy doll, she climbed in the chair with Don and fell asleep again. Kathleen walked in from the back room and headed straight for the coffee pot. After pouring a cup she added cream and sugar and was slipping away. Danny had also strolled in and spread out on the couch across the room. When they had got there the night before everyone was fired up about the snow on the mountains all around. After they woke James they all went to the slopes.

For the most part Don and Allen stood at the bottom of the hill filming the rest of the group climbing up and sliding down the Slope. Kathleen and James were the first to the top. Danny had started out with them but it was not long before he was left behind. Grace was with Doris over to the side building a snowman and had asked Don for his hat then his gloves to keep the snowman warm. When Danny reached the top Kathleen and James had been up and down the slope several times. Danny had decided that on the way down the hill it would not hurt to have a snow ball so it could be thrown at any one he should pass as he flew by. He had seen James and Kathleen hit a target or two and thought he might give it a try.

When Danny first took off he did not get far. He had started in an area where the snow had not been packed enough. He moved further down the slope and the sled almost slipped before he got on. When he took off he abandoned the snow ball idea just to hold on. As he went flying down the hill his only hope was that he would not lose control. He had past his brother and sister standing half way down the hill. Then he passed the snow man a little further down. Then at the bottom of the hill and then took air after hitting the bump that separated the hill from the snow covered parking lot. Danny survived the impact of the crash but the sled however did not. Allen and James picked up the pieces they went home to get warm. That evening Danny and James played Jenga, Kathleen and Doris played scrabble, And Don and Allen played monopoly all night long.

The next Day Kathleen went into the back room to

wake James up. She had been back there for almost ten minutes before she came running out like she had seen a mouse. It was not long after James came out running behind her. He chased her around the living room and out the back door and Kathleen then was diving in the snow after being pushed by James.

When they came back in, everyone was staring at them waiting for their explanation.

Kathleen said she had tried all the conventional ways to wake James up and when none of them had worked she had used a snow ball instead. The room was filled laughter at Kathleen and James reenactment.

Later Allen asked Don if he had heard from Addison since he had been back in town. Don said that he had thought about her but she had left with her church today. He did say he wanted to make contact with the Lusters and he asked Allen when they went home if they could stop in to see them. Allen agreed to the detour and they spent the day relaxing while watching the snow fall from inside

After the day of excitement on the slopes that they spent time at the at the lodge the entire day. Kathleen was buried in crossword puzzles, James and Danny playing monopoly. Doris, Allen and Don had a very intense game of scrabble. The loudest noise in the room was the background music from the weather channel. Don had a newspaper from the local store and was skimmed through it between turns. He read an article on the back page that explained why the mountain they were on was so deserted. It was a protected land mark reserved for the Navajo Indian tribe. They were the first tribe to come into New Mexico a hundred years ago. James spoke up at the thought that they might have so kind of curse on them now. The day was filled with fun and excitement but afternoon soon turned to evening most of the games were put away however the monopoly game continued.

Don, Grace and Allen had been outside while the steaks were cooking on the grill they were reminiscing about old times. Don was telling Allen how much he loved his family. They both agreed that letters and phone calls were nothing compared to being together. As Allen flipped the steaks he noticed the chill in the air had deepened more. Grace had gone in to worm up and Don had buttoned his coat and was blowing on the ends of his finger to keep them warm.

As the evening progressed the thermometer went further and further down. Soon they were all at the table inside. As the night went on some of the games were pulled out again. James and Danny had left the monopoly game out, and picked up where they had left off before.

The next morning Kathleen, James and Danny were found sacked out in the living room in front of the fireplace, when Grace came in and saw them she laid down on next to Kathleen and snuggled in close. The trip back to Indiana was not until later that day thus there was no harm in letting them sleep on for a while. When they Did leave Don talked about Addison and what he might have missed there. Allen thought back to when he had met Doris for the first time. She had come through Lubbock not even planning to stop but because she had Allen was never the same again.

Allen recalled the letters he had written to her that

seemed to be proof that the goals they had in life were one in the same. He knew that he needed to go to Indiana to see Doris he need to know if this was the real thing. As he talked to his brother about it, Don had agreed if he was as serious about Doris as he let on, he needed to find out if she was serious too. Allen could not get his mind off her he had looked for her in all the same places that he seen her the year before. All the letters he had written seemed to come so easy however now he did not know how to say what he was thinking.

Don drove past the Indiana state line and blew the horn of the motorhome. It would not long now until they reached the Lusters. They all were looking forward to the visit again. While Don Drove Allen and Doris were busy making beds and cleaning the camper and gathering all their junk. Don was wanting to get to the Lusters before dark he felt bad about leaving so abruptly he wanted to do some of the chores he had promised them in the beginning. Don and Allen were up front Doris was playing rummy or rather teaching rummy to Grace. James was still doing his best to hear the truckers on the other end of his C b radio. Danny was looking out the window counting the cars as they went past him, and Kathleen was standing at the stove trying her best to cook the hamburger helper while going down the highway.

Bouncing around the motorhome while it was moving was not as hard as Kathleen imagined but as she put the cheese and burger mixture in the disposable bowls one bowl for everyone, she moved around the camper with a surprising ease. As she gave the bowls to her Mom and Grace she had somewhat of some mixed feelings.

She loved her new cousin and thought she would give up anything for her. Although when it came down to it having to share her mom was harder than she thought it would be. Grace did not know it but she had invaded on a sacred tradition of rummy that until today only Kathleen had with Doris. Kathleen finally decided that some things were worth letting go of and she loved Grace more than her rummy games. She then decided that although the rummy game must go on, there was no harm in adding a player to the game. Kathleen sat down next to Grace and the next hand was dealt to her as well. As Kathleen sat down Don had glanced back to see the interaction. Allen had seen Don's stare and followed his gaze.

Kathleen had always wanted a little sister. Neither Allen or Don said anything but Allen could see that he was beginning to cry. Just then they heard Danny yelling from the back of the motorhome Allen got up from the passenger seat to see what he was yelling at.

"And now ladies and gentlemen, it's time for the race of the century."

Allen peeked over to see that Danny had six of his matchbox cars lined up at the back of the motorhome with a ruler in front of them. Allen put his hand over his mouth to muffle the laugh. Danny pushed the ruler, and screamed louder.

"Blue starts off in the lead, oh but wait yellow is getting close, oh red crashes off the side. Better luck next time green, purple and black are neck and neck, and yellow take the lead just before the finish line to take the win."

The finish line was the table where Kathleen had

been sitting, a few seconds later Allen saw the yellow, and then the blue and green cars roll into his shoes that were between the seats. After waiting a moment to watch for more traffic, he made his way to Danny. He stepping over the purple car he almost slides across the floor on the black car, as he walked over he saw the red car off to side.

After that everyone clapped their hands and Danny took a bow as he crawled across the floor to collect his cars. When he got to the blue one he mumbled that it needed a tune up. Allen heard that and asked Danny if he could give his old truck a tune up when they got home. Danny reminded him he only did the small ones and the big trucks were his job. Allen then said that maybe Danny could give him some pointers at least.

His truck had never run as good as those cars. Apparently they were not supposed to, Danny said. Match box car were always going to be fast, and Danny was not even sure that the old truck would even start. He then further explained that his red car was actually fast as well it might of won had it not of turned his wheel to fast and flipped over. Danny was going to have a chat with the driver and encourage him to hold her steady on the next run.

Everyone's attention had been on Danny and even Don was watching from the rear view mirror. They all were laughing hysterically, Danny was just trying to entertain himself and it became their entertainment as well. Allen had made his way back to his seat they were passing a hay field. Doris saw a couple riding horseback along the dry grass parallel with the road. As she focused on them it was clear to Allen where her mind had gone.

One of Doris's dreams was to ride off into the sun set on horseback on her wedding day. So when that day came Allen made it his business to make sure her dream had come true. However, exciting as it was to ride a horse they did not want to ride the entire one hundred miles that it was to their bed and breakfast. They made plans with Don to put the car at a farm across town. They would leave horses there and drive, the rest of the way. When they got across town to get their car someone hid the keys in the hay bale.

Don would argue the point to his dying day that because he left the clues on how to find the keys in plain sight that they were not actually hid at all. He had the haw bails stacked in a stair case and the key were on the top bail. Doris had more fun with it than Allen did at the time. It however made the mattress of the bed and breakfast feel pretty soft. The thing that Don had always kept in mind was in meant that when he found that special girl that it will be payback time. He would just have to make sure there were no horses nor hay bales at his wedding. Passing the hay field meant it was only another five miles to the Lusters.

Don had been telling Jokes the whole trip and when he realized that they were almost there he had to throw one more in. This one was about the spices. They had worked all morning putting flavor in the food the chef finally decided he was going to lunch. It was here that the spices wanted a party.

The plan was to have the black pepper stand guard. The signal was he was going to sneeze when the chef was coming back. Time went on and they were all partying away having a good time. It was in the middle of the limbo game that the peeper saw the cook coming back he started to run to his place on the shelf as he did he remembered he had forgotten to sneeze to alert to others. Instead he called out to them

"Are you guys cumin?"

"Yah but we need more thyme."

Everyone except James sat in silence with a blank stare. Allen and Doris pretended to cry, Kathleen shook her head, Grace did not get the joke, and James thought it was a cool one but still shook his head while he laughed. Danny was at the other end of the motorhome racing his hot wheels. James asked if he had another one. James was given a stern look from everyone else. Don told James never to go to a fruit stand and ask for ate apples and them complain because that one of them has a bite taken out of it.

ICE CREAM SHACK

Don pulled into the Lusters Drive way and every one jumped out without a word. After they were gone Don stayed in his chair to take it all in. Tears began to form when he saw Laura hugging Grace. Quinn got down on one knee and told Grace he thought there was little girl coming and there obviously was some mistake because she looked as she was almost as tall as him.

While Quinn was talking to Grace the rest of the group were giving their greeting to Laura. She then turned back to Grace and Quinn turn to say hello to the rest of them. Laura moved to the porch swing and had asked Grace to join her there. Quinn then took Allen, Doris and the kids into the house while Grace and Laura stayed in the swing.

It was her that Quinn told everyone that Adison had not left with the rest of her group. Quinn then said that he did not wanted Don to know until Adison could tell him in person. Allen grinned and rubbed his hands together anticipating the moment when Don came in.

Laura and Grace continued to talk about everything from cabbage patch kids to pet dogs and Don continued to stare from the window. He was still trying to believe that a year ago he had none of this. He dried his eyes and tried to compose himself before making his way to the side door. As he stepped out caught another glance of his daughter with Laura. Back in side Allen had devised a plan. He had decided that they had to pull his chain a little bit at least.

Don, Grace and Laura walked in together and Quinn, Allen, Doris and the kids were a line to blocking the view to the living room. It was Laura who began to giggle first. After that Adison began to laugh as well. She then stepped out from behind the line holding the pie that he had sent to her the day before. Don was silent, he had opened his mouth several times but nothing came out. Starting with Laura then Quinn and eventually the rest of the family, one by one began to leave the room.

After they were alone Addison put the pie on the counter and reached in the drawer for a knife. Don sat at the table and Addison sat across from him. She then sliced two pieces of the berry pie. Don finally managed to say that she had not gone to South America. Addison just nodded her head. The rest of the family had gone outside and Laura was busy chewing Quinn out for listening in.

He had noticed the open window of the kitchen and was trying listen in on Don and Addison. Quinn told Laura that they were only talking about pie. Laura then said that he still should not have been spying on them and he should come to the yard with everyone else. He stepped away from the window but protested that his Dad had listened to them when they were courting. Laura said that it did not make it right and they joined Allen and family at the benches in the yard.

Addison was just beginning to talk and she stopped and turned her head. She then said heard her Mom and Dad talking by the window. They were silent for a moment until Don asked her if she liked ice cream. Addison nodded her head and off they went. As they got up Don offered his hand and Addison. They walked outside and joined the family there for a bit. It was not however the original plan but Grace had given Don her seven-year-old puppy dog eyes and had asked him to be pushed on the swing. Addison was making contact with Kathleen and the boys. Allen, Doris, Quinn and Laura sat on a bench off to the side.

When Don and Addison left they decide they would take their time. It was only a ten-minute drive to the ice cream shack but they were looking at the scenery along the way. Addison pointed out several landmarks as they drove by. There was the street she had learned to ride a bike, then the church she had gone to for several years. They also went by the playground that she went too as a child, and the stables she had learned to ride a horse. After they circled the town for the fourth time they sat down to order their ice cream. Adison had strawberry and Don a rocky road. Addison then began to elaborate on her past.

She was nineteen when she graduated from high school. She had tried several subjects in college but had a hard time figuring out what she wanted to do. When she was eighteen her parents had taken her to see a live performance of pride and prejudice. Before the play began she was awestruck at the oil paintings they used. It was art that she had only seen in books. Addison got a replica of one of the landscapes of the play and she had decided it was what she wanted to do.

She still had couple months of high school left but

she was fired about painting. She said that the first part of the class was interesting they went through the basics of painting. That part taught them how to choose their paint brush and other equipment. Then they went into making the sketch of their painting first after that was color wheel. The next thing was the idea of how to put motion into their art. Adison loved all the theory until she had to pick up a paint brush. She did find out that she liked to write in that class. She had an assignment to put down in words what she would paint and which stroke of the brush she would use

Addison felt that assignment was the best part of the class and it encouraged her to press in and at least give the semester a shot. She eventually transferred out of the class to a creative writing class this class was interesting but Adison was having a hard time admitting that she was not keeping up. It was about his time she had heard about the group from my church going to South America.

Don asked her what South America was like. Adison told him that there were no indoor stoves and all the cooking was done on an outside grill hot plate over an open flame. The houses were bamboo huts and she slept under the stars every night for the first month because the flood had washed away so many of the huts. They were so busy helping to rebuild homes before that they were not worried about where they slept. Addison said she liked sleeping under the stars so much that even after they build a larger structure for the missionaries Addison still slept outside.

Addison was only going to be there for three months but she found out some of the natives had a ham radio and we were able to coordinate contacts to the states. Addison was able to make contact with Jack and then to her parents through the radio. They would talk weekly with them. For Addison every time an opportunity came up to stay longer She took it.

Three months turned into four. Then four months turned into six. The next thing she knew a year had gone by. Addison was aspiring to be a writer and she kept a journal every day. She would periodically read them back to herself to see what she learned. Addison the told Don about time She was out swimming in one of the lakes and one of the natives asked her if had seen the crocodiles yet. She was never to fast of a swimmer but you would have seen a yellow and black blur if you had watching her run.

Don said his grad year was not quite that exciting. He was raised in west Texas as a farmer's son. From the time he was eight he was taught to work the fields. The work was so much by sixth grade year he was home schooled so that he could do the work in the daylight and do his schooling bit by bit here and there. When his dad got a job as a Dallas County Deputy and their parents moved, he was eighteen years old so he stayed in Lubbock. Allen and Don had been doing a good bit of the work because their Dads heart was slowing him down. Don said thought the biggest impact was the transition from Mom's home cooked meals to burgers and hot Dogs but apparently they survived it.

Don also told Addison about growing up with a mom who worked as a sectary for the Hela temple. Every time the circus came to town they always got to go free. He told her how much work it was to climb up on the elephant to get a ride. He also said that there was a five-minute list on how not to fall, and what to do if you did. The view was pretty cool once you did get up there. He also told her that if she ever had a chance to ride one not try it Indian style and that it might have worked in the movies but not in the real world. He also told her about the stunt motor cycles as how fun it was to watch them do flips and tricks around the arena. Everyone that went to the circus got a program book it told who the performers were how old the animals were and sometimes where the bathroom was. When Don was seventeen he opened his book to find a twenty-dollar bill. Don stood and offered his hand to Addison. She took it and stood herself. As they walked out Don said that he wanted to go to Jack's shop and get some two way radios for James.

GETTING TO KNOW YOU

When they walked in the electronics store Addison looked up at the bell that hung over the door. The familiar sound that she had heard for the last thirty years was always the same. Jack was in the far right hand corner of the shop hanging phone cords on the wall he had heard the bell but did not want the cords to get tangled he yelled out loud that he would be right there. Before he had a chance to turn around Addison and Don were there instead. Addison had never been much for electronics but had many times come in with her dad. Quinn had always been able to make his Daughter laugh but he had never seen that certain spark in her eyes like he saw today. They walked up to the front of the shop and Don told Jack what he wanted to get for James. Jack smiled as he thought about how excited James was about his Ham rig.

Jack then went to the other side of the store to a display of family band radios. Don and Addison had followed him and were now picking through the different models they were in a variety of sizes and colors. When they got back to the counter Addison handed him the envelope that he had given her before. She told him that they were in town for several days and she thought that he might want to give it to James himself. Don crack it a bit to reveal what was inside, with a curious look he just nodded his head.

Jack had ordered it the first chance he got. The rules had just changed on the Armature radio license and that created a license that did not need Morse code. Addison offered to invite jack to dinner. He could then hang out with Quinn as well and just have a good time. Don had been flipping through the book trying to make since of all the terms. There was ohm's law, packet radio. There were questions like How many volts are equal to one kilovolt? Another one was Which of the following is an advantage of HF vs VHF and higher frequencies? Don closed the book and turned to Jack to make a deal with him about James.

Don stared off agreeing with Addison that he too would love to have him over for dinner one night. He said that had promised Quinn and Laura that he would make several trips to their house in the next couple months. It would be easy to bring James down on one of those trips.

Jack put the book back in the envelope and puts it under the counter. He told Addison and Don that he would love to have dinner with them. It would be nice to catch up with Quinn and Laura. Don held up the radios he was about buy and asked Quinn if he should wait on those. Quinn told him that he might actually get some use out of those at least until he passes his test. Don paid for the radios said good bye and they were out the door.

But before he got out of the parking lot he had another idea after consulting Addison he headed to the Lusters to initiate his plan. The first thing he had to do was talk to Allen and Doris and get their ok. Both Addison and Don were laughing at the thought of the fun James would have if this idea worked. When he got out of the car he was met by Grace. She had been on the swing but almost leaped out of it when she saw Don and by the time he had his feet on the ground She had latched onto him. Adison just laughed as she looked endearingly to Don. Kathleen had been pushing Leah in the swing. James was helping Danny dig holes in the dirt. Allen and Doris were on the porch swing and Quinn and Lara had gone for their afternoon nap. As Don glance down at Grace still latched to his legs he realized that his original plan of leaving Grace to return home with Allen and Doris might not work as well as he thought.

Don told Allen that after the ice cream shop they made some extra stops as well. Allen said that it was fine. Grace had been having the time of her life on the swing, they have not been able to get her off since he had left. Don told Allen and Doris that when they left later that day that he was going to stay behind. He then said that he would like to keep James with him. Doris and Allen both Agreed and asked if he was going to help with the chores. Don told them about the plan they had made with Jack and they both said not to spoil him too much.

Allen could drive the motor home again and Don would bring later James in Addison's car.

Allen and Doris both are happy about the fact that James get along with Don so well. He then said that as his Uncle it was his duty to spoil his nephew. He then added that Jack was going to spoil him a fair bit as well. Allen Don Doris and Addison all are laughing now and Grace has retreated back to the swing. Don slowly begin to feel the circulation flowing back into his leg.

Don then said that he could keep Grace with him but it was up to them to decide. Doris said

That she had already promised her that they would include her in the lady's day that Kathleen and her do. We can do that tomorrow and she would not even know you were gone.

That just about did it, the girls would have their day and Don, Addison and James have fun with the radios and Danny and Allen will be on Grandpa duty. Quinn and Laura walk out and Allen and Doris get up to offer their chair. Quinn waves then back down and the sat in the chairs on the other side. Allen then called James over. James tosses the shovel and ran towards them. Danny follow and soon after Grace and Kathleen.

Allen had asked Don if he wanted to tell James the news and he nodded his head. When James got their Don asked him if he had enjoyed talking on the radio in the store when we were here last. James replied by telling the whole story over again and how cool it was to meet someone Texas on the air. Don continued by saying that he had been invited back to talk on it again. James handle this news well by doing a big yeh ha as if he was in the general Lee jumping over a sheriff's car.

When James stopped long enough to see everyone was staring at him he pulled his act together and quietly asked when the event would take place. Everyone stop to laugh. Don then told him that he would take him tomorrow or the next day depending on what was going on. James eyes about popped out of his head he was so excited. He was told that Instead of going home with his parents he would spend the night there with Don. James is literally leaping in the air he is so excited. Don then said that If he did not want to that he would stay there without him. James did not even hear Don say anything he was too busy doing a three-sixty spin in the gravel path.

Allen turned to Danny and told him have some time with sissy on the way home and tomorrow it was just them two. Danny did a happy dance of his own it had been a while since the two of them spent the day together.

It was not long after this that Allen had gone and Don was taking James to the ice cream shack. Addison was still trying to work out how she felt about Don but one thing she did know was every moment away from him seemed to hurt more. She was the one however that decided stayed home while Don took James she knew that the guys need their time together too. Now she was at home, alone with her Journal. Her pen hovered as she wondered what to say.

Here I stand drawn even more to you, all I can say is that I want to give my heart to you.

I have found that there is something worth living for now. I give everything to you.

As I look at you I see your heart staring back at me This is meant to be, I can feel it.

I do not know how to explain it however; I suppose if I had to explain it, it would not be true.

My only hope is that you can somehow feel the same way for me. You have brought sunshine and beauty to my life. How is it that I feel both laughter and pain? I wish this wasn't so confusing

My heart is restless yet I am at peace

Addison put her pen down the thought of writing

letters to seemed strange considering she could not bring herself to give them to him pouring her heart out was one thing but exposing that part to Don, not quite that far yet.

Don thought about the fact that he had left Addison behind but then he decides that the tie with James was needed as well. When they pulled in the parking lot Don asked him what flavor he liked, James said he wanted Chocolate. Don said back to him that there was not anything else.

Back in Cloverdale Grandpa George was waking up from a twenty-minute nap. He would never admit it but as much as he barks about wanting to be left alone, he wonders when they are going to be home. Doris did have plans to have the neighbors check in on him but George had been insistent that he would be fine. She had protested that she was not going to leave him here alone all day. George protested back that yes she was and just because he was an old man does not mean that he can't manage on my own for a couple of days. Doris had given up.

She did tell him to stay here in the house where all the food is so she did not have to worry about him coming back and forward all day. George agreed and sat in the chair that he had adopted as his. George got up to refill his glass of tea and heard a car pull up to the door. George knew it was too early for Allen and Doris to be home so who could this be? As he opened the door to reveal the identity of his unexpected visitor he could not believe his eyes. After about ten seconds they were hugging each other and for the next three hours George had been beside himself going over the old times with his guest. They were laughing the entire time about the response they knew Doris would have.

Allen turned down the road that led to their house with the sun now low enough to be in his eyes Doris commented on her dad being left at home. She asked Allen if he thought it was right to leave her dad here alone. Allen said that they were not going to get him come with us.

Allen said that her Dad probably enjoyed the peace and quiet and that will be gone as soon as Danny walked in the door. When they drove in the gate they were greeted by their dogs running around the wheels of the motorhome, Allen slowed to make sure he could see them. Danny had been moving from one widow to the next looking for the best view of his four legged friends.

After They drove into the gate Allen stopped and told Danny that he could go.

Danny ran from the back of the motor home and out the side door before long he had caught up with the dogs. It was hard to tell if he was chasing to dogs or the dogs were chasing him. Grace had taken over the role of going from one widow to the other to watch the fun outside. It was just about dusk thus it was hard for Allen to see where Danny and the dogs were from time to time so Allen was relieved when he got to the house and they were already on the pouch.

When they drove in Doris and Allen were fixed on the strange car that was parked off to the side. They both wondered who it could be. She did not think she was right but Doris had a thought of who it might of been.

AN EXCITING DAY

Inside Grandpa heard Danny jumping up the steps. He got up from his chair and went to the door to meet them. He shook his head and thought how funny it was that Danny always moved at high speed wherever he went.

When Allen got the pouch Clyde was already sacked out on his bed Pumpkin however was doing circles on the porch just waiting for the next person to be willing to run across the yard with him. He was disappointed when Allen, Doris, Kathleen and Grace all walked by without even a hello. He stood at attention watching the door for a few moments more he then laid in his bed but it was ten minutes later before his ears stop standing on end. When Doris walked in she dropped her purse on the floor to embrace what she had seen. Her Uncle David took her completely by surprise. Doris had just been standing there and she finally managed to ask him what he was doing there.

His reply was that he had told her that he was going to come but he never actually did say when it would be. He then made some joke that he came to rescue George from being left alone.

Doris just stood there with a smirk. Then she argued the point that she had offered to invite company over for him but he was not having it. George was not going give up on the first time in three months he was going get some peace and quiet. Doris knew there was an extra room for David in the cottage that Don had been staying in. While he was gone Grace would be staying in the house. George and David would have the place to themselves. David was introduced to everyone in the room and then he started to move himself as well as George to the back house. George had been looking forward to his own place again. He had loved being with the family, however he need a much slower pace.

When David was done getting everything moved he came back to Allen's so George could get a nap. When he walked in Doris was going through the pantry trying to come up with a meal. Allen stopped her with one hand and picked up the phone with the other. He then dialed the number for Domino's pizza. He ordered a large pepperoni a large meat lovers and a medium Hawaiian pizza. He told the driver that his address was 227 Wildfire he also said that they were just down the road from the playground on the edge of town. He hung up the phone and said the dinner would be there in fifteen minutes or less. David pulled out his wallet and said that tonight it was on him.

Allen gave him a look that just wanted to make sure it was okay. Allen had never been above letting someone else pay for dinner. He also did not want to impose on David. David Gave him a look Back that seemed to say Don't try to stop me. He seemed determined and Allen was not invested in pushing the point so thus when the pizza came David paid the bill. That night Doris, Kathleen and Grace were making plans for their day on the town, ever since

Doris had mentioned it Grace had been bouncing off the wall with excitement.

Don had tried to talk Addison in to a quiet dinner for two, Quinn and Lara had agreed to take James for the night Addison insisted on making the meal a family affair. She turned to James and asked him if he wanted pizza or burgers. James stared for a moment as if he was pondering the choices then as if there was no other choice he said burgers. He then added that he had assumed that there would be fries as part of the deal.

Quinn said that he was sure that he could find an upscale restaurant that would have burgers and fries. They might even have soda as well. James had finally figured out that he was being harassed and all five of them were getting in the car. Don Sat in the seat next to him in the back and told James that they apparently did not know who they were dealing with. Half an hour later they were walking into five guys ready to eat. Quinn had been right after all. Not only did they have burgers, fries and soda they also were known for their bags of Peanuts as well. After they had Dinner Don left James with the Lusters and took Addison out for a drink.

The next morning Quinn and Laura sat together in the living room talking about Don over breakfast. Quinn had just come in from the outside with all that had been happening the question of all the work that needed to be done had still not been answered. Laura Knew the Idea he had he Daughter was going to love. She thought Don would just bring all his animals there. Quinn thought it would be best just to wait until they were together.

Just about then Don and James came in from outside.

The first adventure of the day was they had spent the night in a tent outside. It was also the only place to sleep with no extra rooms in the house. They both made their way to the stove and warmed their hands over the bacon as Don made his way to the coffee pot. Just then Addison came as well, she had just came from her house three blocks away. Quinn is laughing as he watches both Don and Addison go for the same cup at once. James sat at the table with his eggs and orange juice.

Don looked down at the counter and the buffet that Laura had created and decided that he thought it was nice of her to go to all the trouble however a man should not have to make so many decisions at that time of the morning. He took some bacon and grits to add to his coffee and they began to make their plans for the day. Jack will open his shop at nine o'clock. Several of them looked at the wall and it was just after eight. That was perfect. The time it would take to finish this feast and get it put away was plenty of time.

Later that morning when Don drove into the parking lot of Jack's store he could not help but crack a smile. He had not told him that he was bringing James by this soon and he loved the connection that the two of them had. He put the car in park he paused for a moment turned to Addison and then James. He then asked James if he was ready to make an old man very happy.

As they walked in the door of the shop the bell above the door jingled and a minute later Jack yelled from the other side of the store that he would be right there. Don, Addison and James were quit at first. James then went over to the shelf where Jack's radio was. He was disappointed when he learned that it had been powered down. He then migrated over to the counter where Don and Addison were.

Jack finally made it to the counter himself and the expression on his face changed to a smile. He went around the counter to get his package for James. Meanwhile making jokes about who had snuck into his store. James was still disappointed about the radio being off but was polite enough to say good morning. Jack greeted Don and Addison and then set the envelope on the counter and turned behind him to reach for a handheld radio. Then he told James he wanted to show him something.

James was paying full attention now he did not know what Jack had in mind but was eager because of the fun he had last time he was there. Jack turned on the radio and pushed the transmit key. The radio responded with a series of Morse code beeps. This made James lite up even more. Don and Addison were having almost as much fun watching James, as he was being a part of what was going on. Jack responded the interest by putting the radio to his mouth and pushing the button again.

"N7jil this is n5bmu."

There was a moment of silence in the store as well as on the radio.

"N7jil this is n5bmu" Jack repeated over the radio again

This time a female voice came on the radio

"This is n7jil, go ahead."

"Hello Jessie this is Jack over in Shadeland."

"Hi Jack this I am currently in Lafayette."

While all this was going on James was so excited that

you would have thought it was Christmas day. James had been using a C b radio for several years so Jack could have dispensed with the basics of how to work the buttons. He handed James the radio and told him to say hello.

James said hello to Jessie and she told him that she was in a town eleven miles away. She then went on about the basics of repeaters and how the system they were using worked. She was currently on high way twenty-five on her way to Logansport where she lived with her husband Mortimer. She gave a quick description of the two repeater that she was using worked together with the radio that was mounted in her car. She then said her call sign once again and was gone.

Jack continued to explain the reason he could talk so far is on the frequency he then explained the basic idea of a mountain top repeater. James was still so excited about his eleven-mile communication on such a small radio that he did not even stop to think about how it was being done. Jack took the radio back as he explained more in depth about the process of repeaters he said call sign over the air once more and put the radio back on the shelf behind him.

Jack asked James if he enjoy it with an obvious tone humor. He then pulled the book out of the envelope and asked him if he would like to be able to talk like that all the time. James looked at him with an interested but puzzled look. To answer this Jack opened the book and explained some more of what a license would allow him to do. A few minutes later the smile on James face returned again.

Don and Addison watched as his face went from happy to wondering to concentrating to happy and then even more happy. The only regret they had was they did not have a camera to show Allen and Doris later. They however were not anticipating that his enthusiasm was going to away any time soon. Don and Addison both were certain there would be plenty of excitement left to share with his parent's back home.

By noon Quinn and Laura had made several laps around town. The grocery store, the drug store as well as a ten o'clock meeting with their lawyer. As Quinn drove up to the shed, the familiar spot that he had parked for over 30 years. He stopped to stared. First he looked only at shed later everything else around it as well. Laura was looking around as well, she would look out at their land and then back at Quinn again Now they did not need to worry, the land would be theirs forever now. Quinn smiled as he thought of what they had done. The question that they had was how long it will take Don and Addison to figure out what they had. They both decided that they did not need to worry about it. They would see it when they want to. Quinn said that his guess was they already had.

Doris, Kathleen and Grace had been in town for several hours now. They had only planned to have an afternoon event however Grace was so excited when she woke up that Doris extended the day for her. Grace had wanted to go to a book store in town. Doris knew that there was one across the way from the Dairy Queen that they usually stopped at. Bothe Doris and Kathleen made a mental note of her love for books, and Doris made a mental note of how to fit it in the day.

Graces eyes perked as she saw the Dairy Queen. Kathleen giggled when she saw the look on her face. It had never crossed her mind that she would have to share the day that she shared with her mom. As she thought about it, she was looking forward to the day with Grace and it did not matter how much she loved her little brothers. The makeup tips, dress sizes and colors of purses was something she has never been able to discuss with them.

Grace was having the time of her life. They had gone Dairy Queen, the grocery stores and the book store. They were now on the way to get manicures and pedicures. Although the pedicurist was having a difficult time when it came to touching grace's feet. She was like her dad, deathly ticklish and although there were a number of people that had the ability to turn off Grace was not one of them. So as hard as she tried to stay still every time her feet were touched she would jump. The stylist was quick to learn this and the dark blue nail polish that Grace chose was carefully being applied by only touching the top of her feet. The act of being tickled was not the only reason Grace could not be still, her excitement was also contributing to her handy cap as well. Both Doris and Kathleen laughed as they looked at each other. They had been sitting there listening to Leah tell her life story to the woman putting the nail polish on her. The manicurist was a mother of three so she was used to the excitement of such things although some of the story that Grace was telling, was hard to believe. She turned to Doris to make sure it was accurate. Each time she did Doris and Kathleen both nod in agreement with Graces version of the story.

Back at their house, Allen and Danny had set out on an adventure of their own. Allen had offered for George to join them but he had declined stating that he was not about to impose on the father son day they had planned. Having three kids it was hard to get one on one with each of them. Now with Don here willing to share the load Allen could perhaps catch up on the individual relationship he had with each of his kids and today it was Danny's turn.

Despite the fact that it was rarely driven Allen had always kept his precious Cadillac in good running order. Today seemed to be a good time to take for a drive. Their destination was Indianapolis for the anal baseball card convention. Allen did have the option of taking the main highway from right there in Cloverdale. The drive would have taken just under an hour. However, they had the whole day to themselves so the scenic route seemed to be the way to go.

As far as the conversation, when Allen would talk to Kathleen it was usually about boys. James the topic had lately been all about radios. He did however mention a brunette that lived across the field that was about the same age as him. This same girl had lived across the field his entire life and it had been the first time James had notice how close she had lived. When Allen thought of this he was taking his exit for the last 30 miles of the ride. He had put the top down due the sun finally coming out. As they drove in the parking lot Danny's eyes grew bigger the convention center itself spanning over two blocks and the entire building was devoted to baseball memorabilia.

GIRL TALK

Doris, Kathleen and Grace were the only one's home for dinner tonight. Don had made plans to be back in Cloverdale but last minute Addison had decided to come along for the ride and at this point they were still almost an hour away. Grace was playing with the dogs on the porch yet trying to preserve her nail polish until her dad was able to see them. Allen had called an hour before to say that he would be eating out with Danny before they came home. They had a day of being at a baseball card convention and they wanted to finish it off with the polish dogs for dinner. Kathleen and Doris were busy getting the house ready for the extra guest.

The plan was to move Kathleen out to Grandpa's house with him and uncle David. Grace would get Kathleen's room and Addison would take guest room, Don would be back in the camper. The meatloaf was in the oven the only sound that could be heard was the fluffing of pillows, the spray of the Windex in one room, and the vacuum in another. The washer and dryer was going as well. The thing that Doris loved to do for the guest rooms was she would put potpourri in with the sheets as they were in the dryer. She always felt that the smell was a welcoming fragrance

James had not put the ham radio book down since Jack gave it to him. He also was given a cassette tape set along with a new walk man tape player. The cassettes were made by Gordon West an instructor in the ham radio world they were a training companion to the no code Tech book that he just received, also done by Gordon West. Jack had gone through some of the book with him while he was in the store going over the highlights of the hobby. He was now in the back seat of Addison's car reading over the packet radio chapter. Jack had told him that he had communicated with someone in Japan using Packet and that caught his interest right away.

Addison was in the rush to throw some things together. She had almost forgotten to pack her most prized possession. Don had assured her that there were a number of stores along the way to get another Journal, still Addison insisted that only hers would do. Don looked over to the passenger seat as she wrote. She was so intently focused almost like he could see the thoughts circling around her brain, if only he could read them.

Much is deep inside that is hard for me to utter. When you arrived this morning I was flabbergasted, surprised and happy. You did something so beautifully. I am full beyond words for your caring. I was thinking of a berry pie then I saw what you did and read what you shared. I'm your heart in poetry that deserves an inward faith. More than is obvious Quicken as it has been. It will be reviewed and to shatter what is not wandering seeking searching asking Inspirations continually renewed in a heart.

Addison put her pen down and glanced at Don, when she saw him in the corner of her eye as she wrote, she could not help to wondered. What was this thing she felt with Don and secondly how was she going to encrypt how he felt about her? She playfully closed the journal as if she needed to protect he secret thoughts from an intrusion. Don reached out his hand and Addison did the same. As they neared the seven-eleven that was near Allen's house Don turned to James and ask if he wanted anything. He did not say anything because he had his headphones on. He looked up when Don tapped him on the shoulder. Don then told Addison that made a pretty good slushy there.

When they drove into the driveway of Allen's house Addison felt an uneasy feeling that she could not quite explain. The feeling did not go away as fast as she would have liked she did resolve that it was most likely related to how she felt about Don. In the short time that she had known the Lane family she knew that all the members she could trust almost with her life. The thing she knew she needed to do was to find Doris for some girl talk. Now she need to get settled in and see where she could lend a hand. She had been invited as a guest but had always been taught, that it did not matter whether she was a guest or hostess it was always better to give than receive.

James walked up the steps with his head still buried in his book. As Don and Addison reach the porch, Don is almost knocked over by grace showing off her blue fingernails. She had been waiting on the porch with her socks and shoes off to display that her toes had been done as well. They walked in the house together and she told them the story about how hard it had been to stay still when the polish was being applied. Grace then continued with a recap of the rest of the day. With more highlights from the salon as well as the book store and Dairy Queen.

When Grace got excited she had always used he hands to emphasize a point. When she had finished her story she had more hand motions than an intense game of Pictionary. When she was done She sat on the couch and fell asleep almost immediately. Don looked up at Addison who had been sitting across from them in the chair. Addison put her pen down, looked at Don smiled then looked back down at the words she had just wrote.

I have never been so touched by a person before such deep emotion welling up inside a fountain that keeps flowing.

Addison feel herself begin to cry and she quickly got up and went to her room. Doris had sensed that Addison might need to chat about things so she made her way back to the guest room to see that she had what she needed for the night. Kathleen has fallen asleep in that very spot only to be carried back to the same room that grace would sleep in tonight. Don turned as he heard the sound of Allen's voice. He paused and then turns to the couch to pick grace up, as he walks down the hall with her in his arms he began to ponder once again if all this was real.

A year ago he was living by himself and as far as he could tell he had everything he needed. He would have not admitted it at the time but one phone call had changed everything.

If he had told Allen no when he was asked to come he never would have met the Lusters he would not have built the bond that he now has with Allen's kids, Kathleen included. He also would not have met Addison. He still would have Grace, only he would have been laying her in the bed in Lubbock instead of here and he would be doing it on his own. Don knew that had it not been for the visit to Allen's he never would have considered asking him for help with Grace. Don put Grace in her bed he nodded to Allen and went to bed himself. It had been a long emotional day and he was exhausted.

When he woke the next morning the same thoughts were running though his mind. However, what he did not know was Addison was awake too with similar thoughts on her mind as well.

As Addison looked at her life in recent years she felt she had been hitting a series of road blocks. There were several attempts at college and they had all fallen through. There was a chance to study abroad but it came and went faster than she could take advantage of it. She had turned down several jobs before she knew the opportunities she was pursuing would not work out. She felt she was in the place where she need to be right now. She was not just thinking about Cloverdale but emotionally in a place that she could handle all the curves life had given her and still come out on top. She did feel in this house with the Lanes was just like she was at home. The atmosphere that she walked into was so close to the feeling being in her own house that when she woke up she almost forgot she was gone.

Then was the mysterious Don Lane. Addison felt like she was trying to solve a crossword puzzle. However, the amount of clues were far less the lines to be filled in. The only one that she was sure about was a seven letter word for man of my dreams was d-o-n-l-a-n-e. She had turning to her journal increasingly more often since she met Don and today was no exception. Her usual method of her pen hovered over the paper as the words in her mind formulated into intelligent sentences. Today despite a journal entry that only she would see, she wrote it as if she was talking to Don

Dear Don

Thank you for a loving and caring family and your time of deep concern. Let your family that care of us both. I can't verbally express my love for you. I don't know you all that well yet but I do know I am in love. I Can honestly say that I know that I am in love with you. I do know that I am in love with the idea of the man I perceive you to be. Deep within me there is a joy waiting to burst. In my heart I have chosen you and someday I will know it confidently enough to tell you face to face that I love you. Today I will just write it here

I love you Don Lane and I always will.

Her thoughts were interrupted by the smell of coffee brewing in the next room. Coffee had always been a weakness for Addison and so off she went to see what else was on the menu. Today Doris had broken out of the usual mold of the big breakfast and set out cold cereal and pastries She had then gone about the business of some other household chores, Doris stopped the vacuum when she saw Addison come in. Doris then asked Addison if she wanted her to heat up a berry turnover. *Addison had already found the coffee and was sipping on a mug full.*

Addison Nodded her head and Doris told her to just let her know if there is anything she needed.

About the time Doris went down the hall to put the vacuum away Grace came in from Kathleen's bedroom behind the kitchen she was of course carrying her snoopy doll. Addison got up to pour her some orange juice and Grace drank it as she leaned on Addison's shoulder. They both stayed that way for a minute or two while the rest of the family started to come in. Don was first and as he walked in he caught a glimpse of Addison and grace. He was carrying a cup of coffee he had made in the camper earlier after his morning jog. instead of coming to the table he sat on the sofa while he enjoyed the morning paper more to the point the peanuts episode in today's edition Linus had built a fleet of snowmen was marching back and forward in front of them, to give his speech. Together were going to conquer all. They will prevail over the enemy nothing can stop. Linus stopped, his fleet had been conquered, by the only enemy that could defeat them, The sun.

James and Danny had been leaning over Don's shoulder ever since Don started the dramatic reading that He was prone to do. James and Allen had been at the kitchen table with Grace and Addison. They all were fixed on Don's portrayal of the event at hand. He stopped rather abruptly when he realized he had an audience. Then got up to refill his coffee and check out one of the berry turnovers after the irresistible smell of James warming his in the toaster oven he thought it good idea at least try one out. He did not want to rude to Doris who had taken the time to bake the turnovers. It would only be polite he thought to himself. While Don had been entertaining the boys with his dramatized version of the peanuts gang Doris and Addison had put away what was left of the food and then had gone outside. As they began to walk the parameter of the property it did not take long for Don's name to come up.

Addison had been having trouble with the fact that Don had yet to say how he felt about her.

Doris said that it was up to her on how to handle it but she also told Addison that Allen took more than a year to say the words I love you. He said it in many other ways long before that.

When Allen first came from Lubbock he was staying over where George is now, he would have never admitted then but they were both sure that we were in love. It was quite a different thing to understand what that meant.

Addison loosened up thinking Don felt the same way about her. As if she was reading her mind Doris said that she knew Don had feelings for her. Addison's face turned red when she asked how Doris knew that. Doris smiled and she told Addison about the day she asked herself the same question about Allen. Addison was determined to find out how Doris thought she could be so sure. To Doris the signs were clear. When every Done heard her name he almost turns red.

He also becomes about three times as clumsy as he usually is. The thing that she was sure she knew was the look that the Lane brothers get when they're in love.

Addison knew the look Doris had been talking about and she agreed that it was rather cute.

Doris went on to say that she thought the more

confidant Don became about how he felt the more obvious his affection would be. She then said that if he was like Allen he would not say I love you by blurting the three words out all the time.

He could be a person that shows love by buying gifts all the time or just wants to spend every moment he can with you. Allen showed his love to Doris by building a beautiful the manicured pond. It took him six years to finish. It did not matter to her. She had seen the love in the labor that he did. As a wedding gift he had dug a pond, cut benches out of existing trees installed pumps to build waterfalls and defined openings in the tree line in the east and west side so the sun could be seen. The idea had come from a bed and breakfast that had something similar that they saw on their honeymoon and when they got home his promise was that she would have one too.

Just then Allen came running out of the house. He had just taken a call from her Mom and the only thing he knew was that her Dad was in the hospital and She needed to get to Shadeland as soon as she could. Don came running out behind him with Addison's small bag and she follows him to the car and they were off.

THE ABRUPT TRIP HOME

"He has lost pulse start chest compressions."

As Laura sat in the ER she went to panic right away. Se heard the phrase code blue come over the intercom. With all the commotion down the hall the idea of trying to see if it was Quinn's room was not possible. She heard was a nurse shouting that there was an adult male in distress, and the room number that was shouted was the number she knew to be Quinn's.

Quinn had been trying to dig a hole for the fence just behind the house and he lost his balance and hit his head. Laura did not think he lost consciousness but he had been feeling dizzy. So she called nine, one, one. He was taken to North Central health a small clinic size hospital just around the corner from their house.

Laura looked up from the waiting room chair to see a young lady in her twenties standing before her she was wearing grey scrubs and was about five feet tall. Laura got up and followed her to Quinn's room. As they walk down the hall the nurse apologized that she could have not come sooner. She then told Laura that the man in the bed next to Quinn had gone into cardiac arrest. He had been moved up stairs to another room and Quinn had a room to himself now. She breathed a sigh of relief when she realized that it wasn't Quinn that was the one in distress.

She then asked how he was doing. The nurse thumbed through the papers on the clipboard. She told Laura that his vitals were stable and they were going to keep him overnight for observation. It was a precaution that anytime a head trauma is involved it never hurt to be sure everything is ok.

Don and Addison reached Shadeland and Addison began to give Don directions to the clinic. They still did not know what condition her dad was in. When they reached the parking lot Addison jumped out of the car almost before Don came to a stop. It was short jog to the nurse's station. She found the room number and was running down the hall. When she reached the room both her Dad and Mom were fast asleep. She did not want to disturb them she quickly retreated back to the nurse's desk to ask about the condition of her Dad. The man at the desk told her the same thing they had told Laura an hour before. He was stable but because he bumped his head they are going to keep him over night.

Addison sat in the waiting room with Don. Neither one had said anything but their silent thought was wondering what they could have done to prevent the fall. The project Quinn had been working on was one that Don had promised he would do but he had kept putting it off. Don was not completely sure that if had done the hole before leaving with Addison that Quinn would have not found something else that needed to be done however he still felt bad.

Addison had not lived at home in several years but she

visited often. When she came she had always found herself looking around at what had to done, however she had never taken the time to ask what she could do. Addison knew her dad was a prideful man that would not ask for help unless absolutely necessary and perhaps not even then. She had gone off to pursue her dreams and Quinn was not going to discourage her find out what she wanted to do with her life.

The other thing was even if she had been there to help him she knew he would have not been sitting on a chair while she dug the hole. Her dad would never have sat and watching while someone else did the work. She did have some comfort in the fact that if she had been there she would have perhaps been able to prevent the fall. Don looked at Addison to see silent tears were covering her cheeks. Addison realized that she had been holding her breath and took a long sigh of relief. She relaxed and went to the vending machine. When she came back with her coffee she went almost with a fall to the chair next to Don leaned into his chest and cried. She started to say she didn't know if it was a good idea to leave with Don. She however knew that unless she had hand cuffed her dad to the chair that all she could have done was watch.

Both Don and Addison worked side by side through a good part of the afternoon. They were also trying to keep one ear on the telephone. They both were wondering why it wasn't ringing but also glad it wasn't. By the time Four o'clock rolled around the adrenaline from having to rush home had worn off and both of them were in the kitchen sipping ice tea. After some thought of what they could eat Addison dashed off to the freezer.

She pulled out a bag and put it in the microwave. Two minutes later Don perked up as he recognized the familiar smell. It was almost like a meal with three simple ingredients. Sharp cheddar, bisquick mix and ground sausage.

When Laura gave them to Don for the first time he was convinced that they were his new favorite snack. It was not long before they had managed to almost empty the entire bag. While Don and Addison were discussing the genetic makeup of cheese balls Quinn and Laura had been discussing the events of the day or more to the point the contents of three fold pamphlets they were looking through.

You can probably guess that there was a bit of resistance on Quinn's part about the idea of a rest home. Laura however had to try after what they went through that day she knew something had to be done. She thought she might win him over with the fact that one of them had a fancy pool table. She pointed to a picture of the wooden staircase on either side of the front of the building. There was another one that was a Christian run home it had no stairs but they did have a swimming pool. This one had a chapel and a large lawn area. They also have couples living areas so they could retire together. Quinn says nothing but took the brochure from her and looked it over.

He put his hand on his chin then cracked a smile when he read that there was only a ten-minute drive to the limestone national park, famous for their striped bass and channel catfish. Laura was glad the he had found something he liked about place but seriously, when was the last time he went fishing. After she thought about it she recalled that before they moved on the farm he did go to the lake now and then.

Laura went to the nurse's desk to see if they had a plan for him. On the way there she thought that she did not see the fun in fishing. In her mind there was nothing less relaxing than sitting on a boat in the middle of a lake waiting for hours at a time for a fish to jump on a string. When she got back to his room she told him that he had to stay the night but because the other bed in the room was not occupied she was welcome to stay too. There were several other pamphlets they looked at but soon they put them away so they could relax.

Grace had been left with Kathleen when Don had to leave and she was having the time of her life. Kathleen had always been good with her younger brothers and it was that much more fun with another girl in the mix. Grace was having so much fun she could hardly contain herself. She did miss her mom but this was beyond fun. She had as much time with her dad and Addison as she wanted, two Uncles an Aunt, three whole cousins, and a Grandpa. She had Breakfast with Addison and then did makeup with Kathleen and now was hanging out with Uncle David, James and Danny at the Dairy Queen.

Just before they were about to walk in the door James asked her what kind of ice cream she wanted. These kind of decisions were always hard for her but by this time she got in the door it had narrowed down to rocky road and strawberry. She was in the process of weighing the options of the two and rocky road won. However, there was another dilemma of the toppings. She had to decide between chocolate with chocolate sprinkles or chocolate with strawberry sprinkles or chocolate with no sprinkles. After that decision was made Grace had to make another decision as well. Does she want it in a bowl or a cone? While Grace was tiring to decide how to stack her ice cream they were all waiting at the counter.

When they got back to the house Grace had been so worn out from her adventures of the day she had drifted off to sleep. Allen and Grandpa had taking turns pushing her on the swing. She had also done the slide she then tried the monkey bar three whole times. She even sat on the grass with George for a while. She had asked him a lot of question. Some of which were, what kind of food he like had he lived there his whole life and if he had ever been married. George had answered all her question as they came. He was born in Prosper Texas and had met his wife Debra in in a town named Mexia, but moved to Indiana several years ago to take on the farm. Grace had gotten all excited at the thought that she had a grandma too until George told her that she had died when Doris was a child. Grace told him that her mom had died too and it had made her feel better that she was not the only one that had lost someone. He told her that he thought her mom and grandma were up in heaven have a good time together. They were probably carrying on about all the things you did together before she left. The gloomy look dropped off of Grace's face and the spark slowly returned as she thought not only the fun she had with her mom but also the fun her mom and grandma were having.

After most everyone had gone to bed Doris had been busy putting together burger patties for the next day and just about the time her hands went into the bowl of raw ground beef the telephone began to ring. She took a minute to look around to see if Allen was in earshot of her voice but after yelling his name through three rings of the phone she cleaned her hands enough to be able to reach the receiver. After she took the call she hung up the phone and started to look for Allen. She found him outside in the barn putting a coat of wax on his car. Doris stood there in the door way with her hands on her hips waiting for him to notice she was there. Of course how would he know anyone was there with the volume of the stereo on high. He finally did she Doris standing in the corner and turned it down.

Doris gave Allen the news from Don about Addison's dad. She also told him that they were going to be gone a day or two. Allen nodded while singing the words to the song on the radio. After that Doris went to finish her project. Doris had been tired she was not used to all the excitement that an eight-year-old could express and hinted that she might have time for a nap if there was time for such a thing as that. Doris knew however that she was done for the day and she would not appear again until tomorrow.

One thing that David had not told anyone until a day or two ago was the reason he had come so quickly was that he did not actually have a place to live. He was not hard up for money or anything like that but until recently he had been the main sound man for a rock band and moved around with them so much over the last three years he had just decided not to get his own place. However, now that he was here he felt like it was time. It did not seem to him that starting his own family was going to happen any time soon but as he looked at Doris and Allen's kids in the car with him. Well he couldn't have asked for anything more.

They had been to several apartments and all of them were pretty run Down. They were all also too far away from the pizza place. Pizza was very important to David. Danny brought up the fact that it needed to have a good playground. Kathleen said that whatever they did they needed to do it before she had to break out the flashlight to find the place. James was having fun with David but he wanted to get home to his favorite television show He also don't want to be late for his Moms burgers. Danny did not want to miss the chocolate chip cookies that he knew would follow.

Then David told them that he had already found a place. James and Kathleen both turn to each other and then to David. Then they asked why they had been circling town a for two hours looking. He told them that he thought they were having fun and that was all that mattered. They just shrugged their shoulder and decided that they could agree with his logic. David put the car in park and stared to get out then turn and asked them if they wanted to see it. They had been there earlier in the day but he had told them that they were full. He told little white lie because he wanted to see if the place he had picked was what they would have liked and he also thought a little adventure would be fun before his secret came out.

TIME FOR CHANGE

Addison and don were about to walk in the front door of the hospital After Addison and Don finished the cheese balls and iced tea the day before Addison made a call to the hospital to check on her dad. She did not talk long and from Don's perspective it was a series of grunts moans followed by yes, no and ending with a well ok. After she hung up Addison announced to Don that Her mom had asked them to come by. She did not say it was an emergency however she did not want to tell them over the phone either. It seemed strange to Addison but she of course agreed.

When they walked in to room the first think Laura asked was if they had brought the envelope. Addison had long since learned to trust her mom and dad, so when her mom told her to bring the envelope in the desk draw she knew better than to ask what it was. Her mom had told her, that she would see when she got there. Laura put the envelope on the on the table behind her and picked up the pamphlets that Quinn and her had been looking at before.

She then told them about the discussions Quinn and her had been having about assisted living.

They were just ready to be done with having to be so careful every time they want to do some work around the house. At the same time, they love that old house and would have hated to see it go. Quinn handed Addison a brochure for the retirement home it was open to the part that explained couples retiring together and Laura had circled it as well. As Don and Addison began to look through it the realization of what they were thinking came clear as the reality began to sink in Laura handed them the envelope that they had brought from home. When they looked at what was inside their expression went from surprised to amazed and overwhelmed.

Quinn told them it was about time they figure out that they are the only one that cannot see all the sparks and fireworks. He did not know whether they were just not admitting it or they really do not see what was going on there. When they did figure it out they are going to eventually want tie that knot. Don turned his head while Addison's face turned three shades of red before she started to cry a stream of silent tears. The tears on Addison's and Laura's eyes continued and soon turn into a silent hug. A few minutes' later Laura gently pulled away and continued where Quinn left off. She told them that they were not trying to push them into anything they were not ready for. When they were ready they now would have a place to live.

Don had always been taught to be super cautious about how fast you moving in on a girl. It was a sign of respect his dad would always say. He had several times had to clamp down the brakes on how he felt about Addison trying to honor the respect he had for her. He definitely knew that the desire to move forward was there he held back fearing his emotions would sneak up on him and then run away.

Addison knew that her parents were right but she was happy where Don and her were. She was afraid of stepping into the unknown she thought it would bring unforeseen trauma to their relationship. They would recover from trauma but it would take time. They were really in the unknown anyhow and Don stirred up emotions in her that she didn't even know were there.

The real question for both Don and Addison was how long would it be before they were going to come to grips with how they felt about one another. The safest thing would be to take it slow and just let it happen as it will.

Laura reached in her purse and handed Addison four, twenty dollar bills. She knew that the grocery shopping had not been done. She told them to stock it with what they wanted. Addison is hesitant but slowly takes the cash. The expression she gave Don was one of disbelief. However, his expression was not quite as surprised. In the last year that he had known Quinn and Laura he had come to expect such behavior from them.

After Quinn hinted that it was getting late and they ready to turn in Don and Addison made their way out to the hall and out the front door. It had been a day of emotional highs and lows for both of them. From the Scare the day before with Quinn's fall and then announcement from Laura about the house. Then there was also having to look about how they felt about each other was somewhat scary as well. Addison was starting to realized that her parents were having a hard time and were getting up there in age. Addison and Don both decided that the only grocery run they had the energy for was pizza hut for a takeout order. By the time they made back to the Lusters house it was 8:00pm. The first thought on Don's mind was the telephone.

He had not spoken to Grace at all in two days. He was a little worried that she would be upset because he had to leave so soon. Don had been so involved with Addison's parents that it was the first time he had slowed down enough to worry about calling home. When he did get to the phone Allen told him not to worry she had been having the time of her life. Don was relieved when Allen recapped the last couple days. The makeup with Kathleen, the ice cream with David and the story time with George the day before and today Allen had given all of them a hay ride then they took their bikes on a ride all over the town and now she was fast asleep.

Don's shoulder dropped with the relief when he heard how Grace was doing. He then expanded the events of that last couple days while trying to eat a piece of pepperoni pizza. Allen assured him that all was well and that Grace was well cared for. Don then explained that in light of the decision the Lusters had made about their house they would stay a day or two more. Don hung up the phone he looked over at Addison. the blond hair that covered her eyebrows he could not help but notice as it bounced around when she laughed and although she was not laughing at the time it was a site he would not soon forget. When Addison caught a glimpse of Don staring at her and she wondered if he was thinking about her as deeply as she was about him. Here they were in the house unaccompanied after just having been confronted about their feeling for one another. The thing she did know about Don was that he was a gentleman. He would and had also treated her with nothing but respect.

If you want a young lady to respect you, you have to respect her. The words of Don's father were ringing in his ear. He had never forgotten the long talks he had with his dad. Sometimes it was in a group session with his brother, sometimes one on one with dad. Sometimes one on one with Allen. Don thought of how grateful he was that he had an opportunity to reconnect with Allen and his family. It was not only because he would want advice with his daughter and girlfriend but the reality hit him that this new life of living close was good. When he found out he was a father was a shock but having a strong family was making all the difference in the world.

Then he thought of Addison, at one point that he asked himself what it would be like to go back to what it was before he met her. The reality was that he could no more go back to that time than he could go back to the days when he was a child. The difference was he would like to go back to the days of his youth wrestling matches with dad and brother family barbecues. He would never go back to the lonely feeling he had before he met Addison.

The next day Don and Addison went the Grocery store and pickup up the supplies they would need to make it through the next couple of days. They were not sure when Addison's parents would actually move out but Addison knew that when her parents had their mind made up their mind it usually was not long before things started to fall into place. The decision they made had taken them by surprise but it was something about the finality in their resolve that made them believe that it was something that they might actually do.

One of the thoughts that crossed their minds was the idea that they might have decided that because of their relationship in whatever state it was. it was the parent's way of encouraging them to look at what the next step would be. Addison knew that when it came down to it that neither her mom nor her dad were going to summit to nurses and caretakers telling them how long to stay up at night or when to get up. They also were not going to be nagged about whether they had taken medication. But she also knew that she was not going to stop them from moving on. Addison realized she needed to find an apartment complex for her parents. Don arose from his blank stare and turned to agree.

The idea of her Dad retiring cold turkey he thought was as about as likely as Allen giving up his Cadillac for a Harley. He thought the apartment idea is the best way to go. It would be a smaller area to keep clean the yard will be maintained for them. It might even have had an extra room for their projects and he knew her mom is not going to give up cooking anytime soon. Addison thought that something close to the house would probably be nice it might help them not feel all alone. She knew her dad was the one who brought up all the work that he could not do. Addison doubted Quinn would stop all together.

Addison thought shift a different direction she turned again to Don but was silent as she thought of how to say what was on her mind she asked Don what he thought about what her dad said about, tying the knot. There was a moment of silence before Don answered. Her dad had stole his thunder.

Don then explained how he had been taught not to jump to quickly when it came to girls and his parents were old school on relationships and such. Here he was trying to be a gentleman and not go to fast and your dad all but popped the question himself. Don gave a sideways smile as he looked over at her and Addison smiled too but turns as red as a cardinal looking to change the subject Addison looks around for a distraction. They had just past Jacks shop and Addison wanted to go in Don laughed as he turns on the blinkers then moved to the lane to exit the road. As they walked it the door Addison looks up at the bell that hung over the door, the thought of how familiar that sound was, was just a tribute to how often she had been here over the years. Jack was in the back corner of the store when he heard the bell did what he normally did with anyone who came in. he inhaled a deep breath and yelled.

In the few minutes it took Jack to make it to the front of the store, Addison, and Don had made their way up as well. When Jack saw who his customers were his face lit up and his arms went out. Addison and Jack held their embrace few moments before Jack turned and held out his hand to Don. He then asked what it was that he heard about Quinn and Laura wanting to move out of their house.

Addison and Don took a minute to explain their theory of why her parents were wanting to make the change. Jack just laughed and he was certain that her folks have used every means they knew of to get them to realize what was going on there. He used his pointer finger to point back and forth between Don and Addison. Jack said that they were doing them a favor, he knew her Dad was not going to give up doing his own chores unless he was given him a reason to. He would keep working till he dropped dead. Jack thought It was high time he learned how to use the recliner more that the post hole digger.

Don and Addison laughed at Jacks dramatic point of view. Jack thought the idea of trying to make it sound like it was their idea to might have been the best way to go about it. He had known Quinn a long time and well she probably knew as well as he did that he doesn't like to be pushed in to anything. Addison was used to it but Don was taken by surprise with Jacks rather comical analogies Jack told them to sneak some roller skates on him and give him a nudge he would end up rolling right up where you want him.

When they left both Don and Addison were laughing and crying. Jack had managed not only to give Addison a secret method of not making them feel pushed. He had also had used a dry humor that was likely to come out of Jack on any given day. Addison did know one thing though in all the years she had been calling him uncle. Jack had always been able to detect what was need to fill the gap. It had sometimes been soft shoulder for her to cry on. It also was a firm word of encouragement to do the thing she already knew was the right thing to do. In this case it was uncharacteristic humor. Because he knew she had some hard decisions to make and a good laugh was just the thing she, they needed to soften the blow. He really was a great guy.

Don could see that he and Adison were really close.

He has been Quinn's best friend for longer than Addison could recall. At some point he became a stability for her. The funny thing was she couldn't even recall exactly how it all started. She did not tell him her deep secrets but he had always been there for her.

In the small town of Shadeland it was hard not to know just about everyone. When Addison saw the apartment for rent. She guided Don through the intersections then was again petitioned for yet another round of hugs as she walked in the office door. Once again she explained her parents needs and reasons why.

"Oh honey of course your folks are going to live here i just adore your Daddy, is your momma still making that fresh cranberry bread?"

Addison said yes and the older woman said she had to take on of those loaves as collateral for the apartment. Both Don and Addison look at each other and smirk. The women told Addison to get her parents over there today and they could move right in. Addison asked if they could we see the apartment. The woman grabbed her keys, Addison and Don followed her out the door and made their way to the back, they got into an electric golf cart and she took of down the paved road.

The woman loved her golf cart, it made no sense to her to start up a car and fill the air with more unneeded pollution just to get two blocks down the road. Back in the good ole days she just jogged up and down this road. She would also use her bike. Her jogging had to retire." she stopped in front of an apartment there was a small dive way. It was a well-kept lawn with potted plants scrubs and such things scattered in somewhat of a random order.

It was a nice apartment Addison thought to herself. A modest size living room straight ahead with sliding glass door off of that to the left was the kitchen further down was a small bedroom project room. The hall took a right and there was a bathroom and the end of the hall was the master bedroom. Don looked around and turned his head and gave a sarcastic smile to her.

The guest room was big enough for Quinn's models. The kitchen was probably big enough to make Laura happy and it looked like there was room for Quinn's barbecue grill on the porch It seemed like they had all the bases covered. Addison knew she had to keep Her dad stocked with model kits and her mom's pantry full of baking supplies she thought it would work out fine

MORE THAN JUST A HOME

Quinn could not believe what Addison was saying. He was not going anywhere without her telling him where it was. She tried to persuade him by telling him he needed to have a little adventure in life. Quinn's opinion was he had enough adventure getting from the bedroom to living room each day. Laura listened to him for a while and decided she had heard enough. She grabbed her purse and started to walk out the front door and said to Quinn, that he was going.

It had been a week since his trip to the hospital and Laura had been on his heels every minute about how careful he need to be. Don and Addison had told them they had found a place that they would like but that was all they had said. If there was anything Quinn hated worse than being left out of the loop in general was knowing that plans were being made that affect him directly and having no idea what they were. Addison knew, that both her mom and Dad would figure out where they were going soon enough. Unless she decided to blind fold them that is just how it was going to be.

When they got there she did however explain that the trip from one room to the other would be a shorter commute and perhaps less of an adventure to put up with from day to day. It had already been furnished for them. In the living room the sofa was a burgundy color and there was a matching love seat. There was a cherry wood finish on the coffee table and a television in the far corner. The guest room was set up with Quinn's models on one side and Laura's sewing machine on the other and a couch sat in the corner.

The master bed room had been set up with new furniture that Addison found for them. The sheets and bed covering however was Laura's favorite set from her own collection. Quinn did not say anything but went and sat in the room with his models and attempted to hide his tears. Laura stood in the doorway of the bedroom staring silently before she began to cry as well. She did not say anything but she could not believe that Addison had done all this for them. They hug each other for a minute or two and then went back to the project room where Quinn was giving Don detailed instructions about things that needed maintaining on their farm.

Both of them just laughed and left the men to talk shop while Addison showed Laura her fully stocked kitchen. It was a little smaller than the one she had across town but with a slight adjustment it definitely would work for her. Addison knew it was going to take more than a new kitchen to stop Laura from doing all her projects but perhaps this might slow her down at least.

Addison looked at her watch and Laura wondered what she was keeping her from. She had been looking at her watch ever since they got there. She told Laura that she put together something for Don to thank him for helping her with everything. When Laura heard what she had done for him she started to push Addison out the door so they would not be late. Addison tried however to be strategic about how fast they left because she did not want Don to figure out something was up.

Don had come out to look at their enclosed porch he was trying to figure out how to get Quinn's barbeque out there. Quinn and Don both were looking around the living room and porch trying to find the best path for the grill. While they were looking at the gate outside deciding whether it would work to come that way. Laura looking up at the clock and said that she need a nap. Don and Addison look at each other and start to gather their things. As they begin to leave Addison turn and smiled at her Mom and thanked her for helping her out.

Don and Addison drove up to the front of the house the surprise that is waiting for Don was making Addison bubble inside. When they get to the porch Grace came bursting out of the door and ran to him. Before he had a chance to respond Grace was latched on him tighter than the bailing wire of a hay bail. Don started to look at Addison and then Allen and James who had come out the door as well. Don could not manage to speak over his tears so Allen told him that it was Addison's idea. She had thought about how he had dropped everything when the call of her father happened the week before. Don was not very good at hiding how much he missed his little girl and he finally turned to Addison and silently mouthed the words thank you.

They went in the house and Allen caught Don up with the Cloverdale local news. He told him how Grace had been doing and that she had just gotten a new cabbage patch kid. He then said that David had found his own place, and was offering to take the kids whenever needed. Allen loved all the family time but was relieved that everything was settling down. George was also happy that his late wives brother had reappeared but there was a good reason he had a house to himself. There were times that he just need to be alone.

James had been reading the book Jack had given him none stop. It was all he talked about and Both Doris and Allen were glad to see how excited he was about it. When Don was in Cloverdale he had taken Danny and James to several Cloverdale highs basketball games. Allen told him that the whole town was celebrating because they had won the state title. After getting the update from Allen he looked over at the scene from across the room Grace was combing her dolls hair while Addison combed her hair and James was buried in his study book. Don got up and walked over to James winking at Grace as he passed. James looked up and Don took the book and opened it to the question pool in the last chapter. He looked over a couple of pages and then looked at James and asked him if he was ready. James nodded his head with a grin of excitement. Don continued to look through the questions and read one aloud to him.

"Why are UHF signals often more effective from inside buildings than VHF signals?"

A, UHF antennas are more efficient than VHF antennas

B. This is incorrect; VHF works better than UHF inside buildings

C VHF signals lose power faster over distance

D The shorter wavelength allows them to more easily penetrate the structure of building

James is silent for a moment before answers hesitantly

"D" He says almost with a whisper

Don is silent for a moment more but then told him he was correct. Don read another one just to make sure he was not just lucky and he was right again.

"Yes" James yelled as his fist went in the air.

While Don was quizzing James, Addison had been giving Allen the update on her parents move and the house that was now hers. Allen had actually heard everything from Don several days before but he knew that Addison needed to process all that had been going on with her. He listened and let her know that he was there to hear whatever she had to say.

Grace held up her doll and looked at her for a minute or two. She then said she thought Lizzy liked strawberry ice cream. Addison looks over at the doll and asked Lizzy if she was sure on her chose of flavor and made sure that she knew that Grace's favorite flavor was rocky road.

Addison was silent for a moment with the doll up to ear. She then said that Lizzy said that they Should share a double scoop bowl because she liked rocky road as well as Strawberry.

While James is back looking in his book Don and Allen are almost in tears as they watched the interaction between Addison and Grace. Grace then asked Don if she could get some ice cream.

"Rocky road, did someone say rocky road alright time for ice cream." Don replied

Grace straitened up and started to run out the door and Addison Got up to follow her to the car.

Don stopped and asked James if he was coming. He said that he did not want any Ice cream while turning the page of his study book. Don gave sly look to Allen and then told James that he would tell Jack from the electronic store that he said hi.

James was out of his seat out the door and in the back of the car before Don made it to the porch. Addison Allen and Don laugh. They were soon driving down the familiar road into town. Addison was still interacting with Grace from the next seat Don looked back from time to time with a smile as wide as the bumper on the car. Addison caught his look and smiled back.

Addison told Grace that she remembered when she was her age she had such a hard time with all the ice cream choices that, her mom used to play a game with her on the way to the ice cream shop and when she got there each time all she had to do was tell them what she wanted. Addison asked her if she wanted to play, Grace said nothing she went on. James poked his head out of the book he gave a blank stare and went back to studying again. The Game started with a simple question. Addison gave her some things to choose from and all she had to do was choose what she liked the best. First she chose between vanilla, Strawberry and rocky road. Then her choose was Cone or bowl. Don was hoping she would pick bowl he thought of the comes dripping mess that a cone can make in an eight-year-olds hand. Finally, was the choose of sprinkles. When Addison asked her about those she said that it was the hardest one to choose from and she asked Addison to choose for her. Addison and Leah finished their talk about ice cream and then moved on to a discussion of Graces collection of dolls. James still had his head behind the ham book and Don and Allen were sitting up front. They were half way listening to the Girls, but also chatting about things going on in Cloverdale. Addison and Grace had moved on to the outfit that Grace had on it was blue jeans and a pink shirt with white stars on the sleeve. Grace held her arms out to display the.

After reaching town, there was a small debate about whether to divide between the ice cream shop and jacks electronic shop. They decided to keep together and they went to jack's first they did not want the mess of the ice cream on the floor of the electronics shop.

When the bell over the door rang Jack was in the back room behind the counter where he kept an old bed that he used from time to time. It did not take much to rig an intercom up since he was in an electronic shop. From the front of the store to back of store room where he was when he heard the bell he could yell just like he always did as if he was just around the next shelf.

Addison would always just, yelled back to him.

When Jack came out he and Addison embraced almost immediately. Jack had never seen the bothers together and did a double take when he saw them. Don and Allen both saw the confused look he had but they had grown accustomed to that kind of response when they were together. Don introduced Allen and Doris. Then Quinn introduced himself to Grace. He reaches under the counter and returns with a small basket. It had been filled with small toys and hair stuff. He told her that the basket had been saved for the special visitors. He then asked her to hold out her hands. He then gave a hand full of toys and candy.

Don then motioned to Jack at the section of the store that he kept his radios to point out where James had been since they walked in. Jack nodded and headed that direction. The ham rig that James had talked on several months before was not turn on this time but that did not matter to James. He still could recall all the fun he had and the idea that he might do it again someday was good enough for him. He turned the frequency dial flipped a switch or two and even looked at the connections on the back the one switch he did not mess with was the power switch he had his hand on it a time or two but decided it was better not to turn it on. As jack walked up from behind he noticed the familiar color of the ham book stuffed in James back pocket. He said hello and James turned around at the sound of his voice. Jack then told him that there were to many thunderstorms happening at the time and it was better to keep it off for now. Jack also asked James how he was doing with study book. James pulled the book out of his back pocket

And started to ask about ohm's law. Jack said that George seemed to be tripping up a lot of people. James gave a wondering tilted look before Jack explained that George Simon Ohm was a mathematician born in the 1700's that was interested in electricity and current. He pulled a white pocket size pad out of his shirt and starts to draw a circle. Allen, Don, Addison and Grace had been standing off to the side watching Jack with James. Addison had taken Grace to the ice cream store while Allen and Don watch James have his fun.

TIME FOR A SNACK

By the time Don, Allen and James made it to the ice cream shop Grace and Addison were already sitting at the corner table, Grace had realized that her doll had been left in the car napping so Addison and Grace had decided to skip the cone and just share a bowl together. When Don found them across the room they were both using straws to drink from either side of the bowl. After the Three guys made their order they went to where the girls were they each had bowls as well although they seemed to be the extra-large size for each of them rather that the medium that the girls had shared. They all three scoops a piece a strawberry, chocolate and vanilla. Addison looks over and made sure don notices that she is staring at their bowls and then smiled at him. He blinked his eye at her before stirring his three scoops together. The three of the guys had the same three scoops of ice cream however they all ate three totally different ways James was being very careful to eat his scoops separately chocolate first, then strawberry and then Vanilla. Don and Allen had both mixed theirs up trying to get one flavor out of the three but don was waiting for his to melt a bit so he could try the straw idea that Addison had done meanwhile Allen was eating his right away while the scoops were still hard.

Addison looked over at James and asked how his visit

with Jack was. James exploded with the excitement of how fun it was. Jack had told him how to understand the ohm's law. How to memorize the frequency's and he also explained more about the repeater systems. He had said that he knew a team of hams that would test me anytime whenever he was ready. He then said that he could come back any time he wanted to talk radio stuff with him. It was here that James turned to his dad and asked if he could just move down here with Don and help take care of Grace. He could also help on the farm there was still work to be done. Don could also Quiz him ham Questions while he was there. Allen, Don and Addison look at each other and then at James. Allen said they would start by going home and talking to Doris about it first and they would see what would happen.

Addison told James that if he stayed with his mom and Dad and you got the license he could talk to Jack from there. James then turned to Don and asked if would study up so he could talk to him as well. Don had to learn a lot of the tech stuff to be a piolet and he did not think it would be hard to learn what he needed to pass the test. He told James as much and James literally jumped out of his chair. Grace was snuggled up in Addison's lap she had been slowly crashing from the long day and now the sugar drop. Allen told Don that she had woke up at five in the morning the plan was to she was so excited about surprising you she woke up then wonder if it was time to go.

Addison got up and lifted Grace with her then handed her to Don. When they got to the car Addison was there to take her again for the ride home. It was only four thirty when they got to the house but she was sound asleep. Don carry her into the house and Addison darted back to her bedroom to pull back the bed for her. When Don came back Allen was on the phone, dialing the number to his house in Cloverdale.

Doris said Hello from the other end of the line, and Allen told her about the decisions that were made with Addison's parents. He then added how exhausted grace had been and all the excitement that she had been having. He then asked her how her day had been.

Doris said that everything was great there. Kathleen was such a great big sister to Danny ever since they left this morning Kathleen had been by Danny's side. Danny went with her to clean dad's house, then she helped him feed the dogs and for lunch they had gone to sonic with George and David a little while ago they had a storm come in with the lightning thunder the works, so they started a monopoly game. Allen told her that they should be heading home in the next hour they had a few more things to iron out with Don. Allen replaced the receiver to the phone and caught Don going the other way and said that he wanted a tour of the of the path way out to back door. He glanced over to Addison, she nodded in agreement.

He got up and reached for his hat out of his back pocket and then James and Addison are left alone. Just before he left Allen had whispered to James to put his book away and be polite.

The room was quiet for a moment while Addison

fumbled through her mind for a topic to talk about. She finally asked if he like working with chickens. She had noticed that he had taken over the job in Cloverdale. He said that he did like it other than the fact that they sometimes could stink pretty bad. Addison then asked him what was his favorite part living on the farm in Cloverdale was. She then told James about some of the places she had been just after high school. James looked interested when he heard about the bamboo huts in Colombia

Addison then elaborated on more of the south America culture and told him why her church had gone down there to help. She also told him about The ham radio that they had and how she used it to talk to Jack and her Parents while she was there. James looked up quickly to that news. He then told her about the conversation he had with the guy in Texas some time ago.

He was silent again for a minute and she could tell he wanted to say something more so she waited. He finally asked her if she liked his uncle. Addison looked at him with an embarrassed look she stared for a moment almost in disbelief. She had not expect James to notice such a thing but then Laughed.

Addison's mind had been so full with the details of her parents in the last week. There had just been no time to think about how she felt about Don. The real truth was how could she not.

He had been a pillar for her right when she needed it. He had given her advice on the kind of furniture to buy. His shoulder was there to cry on when she was overwhelmed. She also would have never been able to set up her parent's new place without his strong arms. The thing she loved to the most was his ability to come up with the corniest jokes that had made her laugh right when she need to. however, she looked at it she was convinced that he was the man to be here for her forever and ever amen.

Her thoughts were interrupted by James yelling out to king him. He then put his hand up and waved. James asked her if she still was playing, she nodded and he said that she needed to king him. He then asked her if she had been abducted by aliens. She said of course not and he said again, so king me. He then told her that she had been gone for a minute there.

Addison turned her head acting like she was going sneeze but was actually just trying to hide the fact that she was still blushing. Then she said that he may have been ahead but to look out because she was going to beat him good.

Allen and Don had made it around the path for the second time and had been sitting in the camper that Allen drove there. Don had been telling Him about the way the Lusters had confronted both Addison and him about their relationship. Allen in return had been telling him some things that he had learned when he was getting to know Doris The advice had come from their dad her dad. Don then said that Addison had offered him the couch but he thought the motor home would work out better until they tied the knot. Allen then asked if they had made any plans yet.

Don pull a small black box out and put it on the table of the camper then handed it to his brother. Allen looked at it for a minute and playfully put his sunglasses to dramatize how nice he thought it was. He asked when he was going to give it to her. Don said that he was going to wait until the dust settles a bit with her folks because he knew It had been taking its toll on her.

Allen folded his arms and grinned then he told Don the they both knew that Quinn and Laura had done everything except drive them to the church in an effort to push them in the right direction.

They walked in the house and Allen called to James that they need to get home so they were not late for Dinner. James gave Addison a mischievous look and said they would never know if she was good enough to beat him and they would just have to count him the winner. Addison that he was the winner right now but when he returned they would play again. Don asked Addison if had heard anything from the back room. Addison said that she had not, however she had not been back there since they got home.

Don looked at his watch and then started to head in that direction, while Addison put the checkers away. By the time Don returned Addison was in the living room with a can of furniture polish making her way around the room. Don stood in distance watching her. When she realized he was there she turned and smiled and he winked his eye.

Jack had given James his phone number and told him he would be expecting to hear from him any day and to keep studying every day. On the way home Allen and James talked about many things the new friends in Shadeland had defiantly impacted their lives. The hard truth was that the visits back and forth were going to have to slow down.

Janes did not say anything but nodded in agreement with his dad. Allen did tell him he could keep studding for his test and when he was ready he would work it out. He followed up with a warning that his other respectability's had better not fall behind. By the time they made it home dusk had settled in but the storm had lifted. Danny along with Clyde and pumpkin had been waiting at the gate and ran after them when he drove onto the gravel drive. Allen stopped, waiting for Danny to catch up. Danny, Clyde and pumpkin all jump in the back of the pickup before he continues on to the house.

It dawned on Doris as they drove in that for the first time in almost a year since all of them were together without all of extra guest. It all had started with what they thought would be a simple one-week summer camp for Danny. George had even found that he liked it better in town that out on the farm so when David offered to give him the spare room in the Apartment, George excepted. At first it took Doris by surprise because he had always loved living off the land. She was however realizing that her dad was no spring chicken anymore and might need a change of pace.

Back in Shadeland Grace finally did wake up about the time the sun went down. Addison and Don had just started on a game of cards and she came in carrying her snoopy doll. Without a word climbed up next to Addison, just to watch them play.

"Addison asked her if she was hungry and grace responded with a nod. Addison got up and returned five minutes later with a ham and cheese sandwich and a glass of milk. Don picked up the conversation where he was just before Grace came in. he had been talking about how he was going to get the stuff from Lubbock. He thought that Allen and him could do most of in the pickup and if need one more trip with his plane. Addison asked him I he was going to bring everything. While cutting Grace's sandwich in half. The only thing he was not sure he could bring was that animals. He would have to sell most of them.

"You're going to sell Lucy?" Leah said between her bites of ham.

Don assured Grace that he would not sell Lucy, she would ride in the back of the truck.

Grace was not up for much longer in fact ten minutes after her question about her favorite chicken she had fallen asleep on the couch. Don decided that instead of trying to take her back to bed he, gave her a pillow and laid her down before moving to the other couch where Addison was. The thought on both Don and Addison's mind was not really said by either one but they both of them thought about the fact that here they were alone now. For the first time without the parents to hover in place over them. Addison at one point had her feelings hurt Because Don would not sleep on the couch or the spare room but as she thought about the man she knew him to be she saw the idea of having his own roof until they were married. It was just another rose in the garden of life they would have together when the time came. She decided not to Press Don about the whole marriage idea. Besides the gentle man that he appeared to be in respect to the matter told her that it would not be long until he made his move anyway.

A HAM WITH A FORK

James had been waiting for his dad in the car but then had come back in the house. He told him that if they did not hurry they were going to be late. The test started at ten, and they still had to meet up with Jack and find the right place to go. He was also going to have to pay a fee and that would take time as well. Allen was trying to figure out what had come over James. He had taken test before but none of them had made him this nervous. Doris said that maybe it's because this is something that he really wanted and not just another school pop quiz. Both Allen, Doris and Don had talked several times about the fact that James had always been interested in radios but just in the last year his interest had peaked. Don had shown up having an interest it, and then Jack showed him some things too and he really had been looking for something to call his own.

When they finally did start on their way to Shadeland James had his book out trying to make sure he knew the key points of the theory. He had been taking the practice tests in the back of the book and he had been getting a solid ninety to a hundred percent most of the time. Allen had spent the last two weeks reading question to James. James had put the book down and was hoping for on last run through on the question he thought he need to know.

He asked his dad to test him a few more times. Allen told him that he was driving and he could not look at the book right then. James then asked him if he would do some off the top of his head. Allen thought for a minute. He then asked James to tell him what was missing from the circle.

There was current and resistance what else did he need. James told him that he had picked one that was too easy voltage was answer. Allen then asked him who the pie chart was named after. James answered that it was Ohms Law, named after George Ohm. Allen did another one this one said what happens when I touch the end of an antenna while you are transmitting. James laughs before answering this one but he then said that he would get scorched.

The next thing Allen said to him was he did not think he needed to do any more and he thought that James was ready for the test. James asked him for just one more and Allen this time stopped to look at the book before asking him how much power to use when attempting to contact a satellite station. James answered only the amount necessary to make the desired contact. Allen waited to see if James was going to pout at the thought of a wrong answer and told him he was right.

They had planned to meet up with Don at his house and they would go to the red cross building across town where the ham test was being held. Jack of course was to be there as with him. While Jack, Don and Allen were going to stay with James. Addison had planned to take Grace, to the mall. Just like he promised when James walked in the front door Jack was there to meet him. They said hello and Jack asked if he was ready. James said of course but the moment he had walked in the door his nerves had hit him. Jack put his hand on his shoulder and said that he was twenty-five questions away from a whole world of fun and excitement and it was all he needed to worry about right now.

Allen and Don had stepped aside when Jack began to talk to James. Jack has done several of this things so he is the best one for James to have in his court right now. James took a seat in the testing room and Jack gave him one of the tests and told him to take his time and just do the best he could. James nodded and then started his test.

Jack retreated to the area where James had seen him before. Allen and Don had come back in and he asked how did with tests in general. They both said that he usually did ok. Allen told jack how confidant James seemed to be about the answers and he had read that book at least three times all the way through. James had even been given Allen a run for his money.

As more people came in and the waiting area chairs started to fill. the doors to the testing room were opened and closed several times. Someone had come out and taped a sign up that read quiet please testing session in progress. They all lowered their voice and sat in the chairs provide in the waiting room.

Addison and Grace were still on their shopping spree. Allen and Don were looking at their watch wondering how long the test was going to take. Jack looked over and told them that he could stay and wait for him if there was something else they wanted to do. They both looked at each other with a hesitation. Jack then told them that he would probably be at least another forty-five minutes and if they can back then. If he was not done, then they could all wait together.

Don and Allen had no trouble getting in touch with Addison and Grace. They had gambled on the way in from the parking lot that they would be one of only about three places. They would either be in the food court the lady's section of Ross or the shoe store. When they did conduct their investigation the verdict they found was they had found a sale on Nike brand shoes and they were busy trying them on for size. After time they decided on a meeting time. Don and Allen went to the electronics store and everyone was happy. For about an hour Addison and Grace went one direction and Allen and Don went another. Don, and Allen were sitting on the couches outside the food court drinking coffee. When Addison did emerge from one store. don and Allen got up to leave only to find out that Addison, and Grace were only passing by, on their way to another store on the other side of the mall. While they waited Don and Allen started to play word games with the different storefront signs visible from the couch. Allen followed Dons gaze to look for the sign. Tippecanoe, was a Battle in the 1800's having to do with the Indiana Territory. Allen then said. Allen looked at his watch and got up to get Addison although halfway there.

Don watch the silent interchange between Addison and Allen. Addison and grace walk back into the store and Allen yells at Don that they were going to go without them. Don caught up with Allen. The girls apparently were having too much fun to be bothered with test results Allen said he pulled the car into the highway watching for oncoming traffic. Allen said that he wanted to be one of the first to see the smile on his face when he comes out of that testing room with a passing grade.

Allen dashed to the door of the red cross stopping short of opening for a moment to catch his breath.

When we walked in he tries to act cool like he has it all together. Jack however calls his bluff.

And said that he didn't miss it. Jack had told him before he went in that if he took less than an hour to go back and check his answers. Jack looked at his watch and said it should be any minute now.

It was ten or fifteen minutes later before the long awaited creak of the test room door started to sound. Jack, Don and Allen all stood as they saw James come out. James knew that there were still others taking their test, so a quiet and respectful as he could do he walked slowly away from the door and ran out to the waiting room but also ran right past Jack, Don and Allen straight outside into the parking lot. They all shook their head and follow him out only to see him dancing in the parking lot. He held up the certificate with the examiners signature on it. Of course they all bust up laughing and ran over to congratulate him.

Jack followed them to a dinner where they had lunch together before going home. Jack went over and was going to go over the logistics, he wanted to remind James of but instead he took him to his shop again and gave him the radio that he had been using to demonstrate with the las time he was there Eventually they said goodbye and were all headed back to the house to rest for the next day.

In the process of Allen and Don trying to pan the seventeen-hour drive to Lubbock to retrieve don's things, they came to the realization that they were going to be gone at least two days. He made several attempts to get Addison to stay at Allen's with Grace but Addison was standing firm on her case that she had a house to take care of now and she was not going to leave. In the end the decision was made to take James up on his offer. He would come to the house stay for a day or two so Addison was not alone. Addison by no means was incapable of being left alone, however not only was it good manners. It also had made James feel like he was giving something to then and also there was work to be done as well. James had always been an extremely hard worker as well as a great asset when it came to helping with Grace. The act was Grace loved him to death similar to the bond that Kathleen has with Danny. Don and Allen had lined him out the day before, there were thing to be done each day as well as projects that were forever going on.

The most interesting job James had to do was with a fork. He would go to the top of the barn with a pitch fork and throw the hay down so he could make bedding for the chicken Coop down below

After a night of driving Don and Allen pulled in to the lot of their old house. They both had a thousand memories flood their minds but it had been a long day of driving and knowing the job that was on their plate the first step in their attack plan was a good couple hours of sleep.

The next morning, they starting with an assessment of what was trash and what was good. There were a lot of mixture of feelings about the definition of trash or not but they had both decided early on that with the exception of a few items like Graces favorite chicken it was going to be a must for the truck and the rest was going in an, all must go moving sale.

When it was done and they started down the road again late that night other than a few blankets and sheets to fill the space the only things they had in the truck was the trunk of Grace's stuff, Lucy the chicken and the beloved and coveted pink Cadillac cookie jar. The owner of the cookie jar was probably the biggest well-kept debate Between Don and Allen, and in their mind the debate would never die. They wanted get to Wichita and stay the night there. It would cut the trip the next day down to thirteen instead of seventeen hours of driving.

This would not only give them a nice break but also if they left at six in the morning like they planned they would be home around nine or ten at night. Allen would then decide if he was going to drive the extra hour to get home or stay at Don's another night. Allen did end up staying over in Shadeland with the plan to leave the next morning in reason was James was sound asleep and the other Allen was not far behind the motor home that don had been sleeping in was a couch too thus Allen and Don were soon fast asleep almost right after they stepped inside.

In the house Addison had seen the headlights of the truck and felt her heart start to beat again. When Don had told her the plan they had to get to Lubbock and back so fast she had tried to talk them out of it and encouraged them to take their time. She did not waste much time pressing the point. She knew Don and Allen enough to know that when one of them got a thought it was hard to stop them however if both of them had the same thought, it was like trying to stop a freight train and you were better off just moving to the side and letting it pass. The one thing that Don did do before he went to sleep was to get Lucy out of her cage he had a pin prepared for her but because he did not want to make the commotion to the barn. He thought it was better just let her loose in the camper with him and Allen. It stood in one place for a minute then started pacing the floor back of the camper. The front of the camper, the back of the camper, the front of the camper, it flapped her wings to get to the counter, she then turns a circle there then jump down Don and Allen watched the parade in silence until they fell asleep.

The next morning when Don woke up, Lucy was on the couch where Allen had slept the night before. As he started to dress for his morning jog he was checking the cupboard for the instant coffee. He had a regular pot but was in too much of a hurry l to set it up he was eager to get to the door to see if he could find the cookie jar from The Back of Allen's truck. However, when he got outside he found the Allen's truck was already gone he could see that graces wooden trunk had been covered and put on the porch. And he was sure that Allen had taken position of the cookie jar once again. As he was jogging his daily mile he was already devising a plan to take possession again. When he came in Addison was already at the stove cooking eggs, stirring grits and buttering toast. He said as he walked up to the coffee pot and she kissed him and asked how late they had come in while she focused on the strawberry jam he said the he was not sure. She knew it had been late. It was the first time she had seen him sleep past eight.

Don took a long drink of his coffee while turning his head to look at the clock, it was almost nine thirty. He asked if Grace was asleep. Grace was convinced that Don was going to get home in time for her to say good night, she had stayed up almost an hour past what she normally did waiting on the couch. Addison motioned to the couch in the front room

He looked at the clock again trying to decide if he was going let her sleep or wake her up. As luck would have it he did not have to decide. Because just then Grace came running out at her usual speed that would knock him over.

PROPOSAL

Don woke at six thirty the plans that he had made with Addison the night before was he would want to go to town before it got to late so he would not have to worry with the heat of the day so she would wake Grace up. Don had made plans with Allen and Doris to have Kathleen stay the night to watch Grace but her arrival had to be timed just right so it was not to spoil the plan he had for the day. He used the phone at Jacks shop to make some of the necessary arrangements.

This was probably the biggest most well thought out plan that he had ever come up with. He went had gone by the Luster's apartment and got what he need from there and then went downtown to start the next phase of the operation. He was taking a chance he knew. Some of the things that were going to take place were depended on decisions that Addison would make. He was hoping he would not need it but his backup plan was in place just in case. The owner of the pizza shop was a longtime friend of Quinn, Laura and Addison. Quinn was at some point in the day would call Addison and ask if the chores he had given Don were being done. He also was going to at the end of the call ask her if she had been by the pizza place in a while and to say hello to the owner if she happen to go. Don also knew Grace loved pizza as well so one word about pizza to her and that was all they were going to hear about. Don thought he would feel bad for working around Addison like this but when he considered the outcome he could potentially have and it made him feel better.

The banquet room of the restaurant would be decorated and set aside. He also asked several of the usual patrons to play along in his game. The real question was would his plan work? Time would definitely tell; Don however would not only cross his fingers but all of his toes as well. The other thing was going to be timing his day so that Addison would not wonder where he was. If it should it take longer than the average shopping trip to town. And lastly because it was obviously a bad plan to use the house phone to contact him about the progress of things he had asked Jack to take his calls there. He would wipe the dust off his old pager from the resort, and he was confident that not only did it work well on vibrate but he could also hide it well in the baggy pockets of his shirt.

His plan was simple, show up at the pizza shop with the appearance that it was a normal Friday night in Shadeland. The crowd that would normally come and go would do just that. The tricky part however was staging the in and out of her friends t, number one so she did not notice it was different but however was all was clear when it was time to reveal his surprise. It was ten-thirty he had been watching the time all morning and he knew if he did not get back soon Addison would start to wonder where he was, so after one last stop he would head home.

Don yelled for Jack as he walked in the door of the shop, when he got closer to the desk he yelled again. He stopped when he saw Jack. One of his arms was up as though to stop him and the other hand was pointing at the phone in his ear. He then continued his conversation with Addison by telling her That yes it was Don that she heard and he had asked him to come by and get something for James that he want him to have. He ended by telling her that he had another customer and better go for now. Jack hung up the phone and paused for a minute.

Then he told Don that Addison wanted him to know that race had drank all the milk this morning.

Don told him that he made a good save and Jack turned to the shelve behind him and gets one of the handheld ham radios and gives it to Don. He pulled out his wallet to pay him. Jack told him to put it away. Jack told Don that if she asked it is a radio with more channels than the other one James had been given.

You just made me a liar to my own niece but I think she will forgive me. Don rolled into the gravel driveway, stepped out of the car very slowly wanting to give Grace time to get to him before he got to the house. He already had a smile on his face because of the activities of the day. He knew her well, forty-five seconds grace came running out the door, and almost knock him over. He then started to challenge her to a tickle war sending both of them into an endless spree of laughter. When Addison came out she quickly grabbed the jug of milk that Don had been holding with two fingers. To further his game Don started to tickle Addison, despite the fact that he knew she was not ticklish. Grace however did not know that Addison was not ticklish and Soon Don and Grace Had joined forces.

When they were done Don reached in the seat of

the car for the newspaper he had bought earlier, the newspaper was a part of his grand plan. He had slipped some advisements for the pizza place in hoping Grace or Addison would see them also the comic section was something actually he needed. Addison knew that Charlie brown always made him laugh. So if he was too spontaneously start laughing because of his plans It could be attributed to the comics and no question would be asked.

The thing he thought about as he watched Charlie brown go flying through the air was, he had tried to devise a plan for getting Addison in a formal dress for the occasion but then he decided just to bring he favorite dressy scarf. She also would be so overwhelmed with everything else that she probably would not even care. As strategically as he could he let the advertisement for the pizza shop slip out of the newspaper. He had although held it with one finger until the time was right.

Grace asked if he could read the comics to her and he of course agreed it was here he let the advertisement fall. He raised his voice a little to try to sound like lucky from the strip.

Grace pointed to the yellow shirt boy she knew was Charlie Brown then they looked at the next slide in the strip and she pointed to Lucy as well. Addison sat in the corner chair and giggled at the site of Don and Grace. He raised his voice before continuing again. Don was asked to read again and Charlie brown again came running up to kick that ball. We all know however that poor Charlie Brown never did get his chance. Leah giggled and

Addison told Charlie Brown never to listen to a women's tears. Don gave her a wink.

When Don got done he made a point of making sure the advertisement is seen again by flipping through the rest of the paper. At this point Don was banking on Grace love for bright colors as well as pizza and together with the other adds that were actually a part of the original paper. It was enough to Graces eye. As she started to look at them Don asked her if she wanted to use the pages to cut and paste. He opened the one from toy r us and pointed out all the baby doll and strollers and asked if she wanted them. She didn't say anything but took them and put them on the other side of her. Don asked her if they could find a bottle or some baby food for her doll. Grace found the pizza shop add, and Don said that would do okay for pretend but pizza was only for the big kids. Grace declared that she was a big kid because she had eaten pizza before.

Addison was still enjoying the interaction between them. She was so involved that she did not realize she was being worked. Don had to back to reading the comics to hide the fact that he was smiling at the whole thing.

Graces was all excited about pizza now. Don said as long as it was okay with Addison and Grace knew the drill, and was already across the room staring at her. Addison looked at Grace then looked up at Don. She then started to talk about the place downtown that Quinn had asked about only hours before She said it was usually packed on Fridays but was great pizza. Her parents had been friends with guy who runs for as long as she could remember. Don asked her if she want to go. Grace nodded her head up and down. Addison said that they might get out of there pretty late if we get in at all.

They decide that they did not care on a Friday night Grace can sleep in all she wanted tomorrow, Don got the phone and asked her what the number was. she told him the number and stepped out the door to make the call. A few minutes later he returned and gave Addison a blank stare. Then Don told her they said it had been so long since he had seen you that if you did not come he did not care how busty Friday night was he would come get you himself.

Addison just laughed and said that it looked like they were having pizza that night.

Allen waited at the corner to watch for Dons headlights to pass before pulling out from behind the huge oak and drove up the gravel road. Kathleen got out of the other side after pulling her overnight bag from the back seat. Allen started to get out to help her but She could get in the house okay and she knew the key was under the mat. When she shut the door Allen taped on the window and waved Kathleen turned around before halfheartedly waving back. Allen waited until she is in the house before he leaves.

On the way to the pizza place Don asked Addison direction several times because they had never been there together. The owner played his roll well and asked Addison introduce Don and Grace to told him. He had bent to one knee when Addison him that She was Don's daughter.

He saw the look in Addison's eye and had no doubt that the twinkle was there because of Don.

He retrieved a coloring book and box with some crayons from the table on the side of the entre way. He then brought two menus and motions with his arm to the table that he had prepared. It was one of the few tables out of plain site of the banquet room. The transition later on would be easier this way he thought. They asked for a large pizza with Hawaiian on one side and pepperoni on the other. They just wanted water to drink and as he began to walk away Don yelled that he wanted jalapenos on the side. He turned back towards him and scratches away on the pad again and the he was gone. Allen pulled into the lot of the pizza place and waited for his cue. Grace had gone back to her coloring book as Addison started to tell Don of the fun times she had there as a child. On her eighth birthday she had a party here and the cake was a dessert pizza with snickers and skittles on the top.

She pointed across the room just to the left to the banquet room. There was more talk about her memories as well as a promise to Grace that her next birthday would be here.

The tray of hot pizza was put in the middle of the table while the bowl of diced jalapenos was given Don. Grace was hesitant to let go of her crayon but eventually the pizza became more important. Allen had his pizza delivered to the car. Some for him some for Kathleen later.

As the evening progressed the conversation went from more stories of Addison's child hood to stories of Dons. There was jokes laughter and question from Grace about everything from the color of the walls and why they were orange to why the bathroom sink was so high with no stool to help her. Meanwhile the owner was watching for the time of his next move. When the time came he approached the table. He asked Addison if she could look at something with him.

She looked over to Don and he nodded okay and got up to join him. He said that he had an idea for a new table setting and he want to see if she thought it would work. Don waited for them to leave before he told Grace he has a surprise for her. He said that Kathleen had come and she was going to spend time together tonight while Addison and him had desert together. He then told her that Allen is going to take her home and Kathleen was there waiting for her.

They went around the corner where Allen was waiting to exchange Grace for his suit jacket. After a thumbs up and a wave and Don headed to the banquet room. Dons hand had been vibrating more than his pager had done all day. When he got there Addison was in tears, the floor of the room had been layered with red and white roses. The lights were all off and candles spread around the room were the only light. When Don came in the waiter had left but soon returned with a large bouquet of flower that almost didn't fit on the table. Don escorted Addison to her seat and pulled it back for her and then sat himself. Having already had dinner the champagne was poured. Don told her he thought they would have dessert just the two of them.

Addison tried to ask what the plan was for Grace but Don said that he had taken care of it and not to worry. He said that he had something for her but she had to close your eyes first.

Addison was too overwhelmed have resistance of any

kind so she just did as he asked. When she shut her eyes he told her not to peak. She said that it was so dark in there she could not see a thing anyway. Don was silent for a long moment them said it was coming. When she opened her eyes it was not the strawberry cheese that she knew to be her favorite dessert. It was a 14 karat diamond ring. For a moment she just stared in silence as her tears started to fall. When she looked up she saw that Don had bent to his knee and she laugh and then cried some more. He reached over and took the box the ring was in and then took her hand he slowly place the ring on her finger as he said these words.

"It's the bounce in your curry hair when you run across the field. The dimples in your cheek when you smile. The concentrated stare when you're trying to decide what to do. it's all of them that make me love you. Addison Luster you have been a shining light in my life since the first time I saw you. You have brought me laughter and joy to the point that I cannot imagine. I cannot go another day without you being a part of it. I am so thankful for the role you play in my Daughter's life, and I cannot truly convey my gratitude. I promise that I will always be there for you no matter what."

The room was silent for a long moment. They stared face to face at each other just taking it in. Addison laughed, giggled and cried until she was almost out of breath. Then she with the tears still in her eyes here face lit up with her smile and she whispered yes to him.and Don began to cry as well.

WEDDING DAY

The time is six thirty, Don had been awake the camper wondering how so many emotions could be felt at once. He was scared silly, amused, happy, excited and over whelmed all at once. He was not normally one to cry in front of others but The rehearsal the day before had made him do just that. He had told Grace that they were tears of joy, and he just so happy that she was there to share the day with him it made him cry. Don laughed when Grace told him that she had promised to throw flour at her. Don told her that she was going to be the most beautiful flower girl in the world.

Don was still laying on the bed of the camper and he thought about the bachelor party the week before and how Allen was able to come up with so many stories to tell about Dons childhood. The announcement about climbing on top of the dog house was not enough he also had to make sure everyone in Coverdale knew that he rode his bike to Idalou, in the middle of the night because he did not like being grounded for coming home late. Don had to correct Allen that it took an hour and a half and not two, like he had said. Don then said maybe it was longer than an hour and a half but he was sure it was not a full two hours.

Don finally got up and dressed in his tuxedo and

headed to the porch where the ceremony was to take place. Grace came running out of the house in her dress. It was a shade of red that was similar to the color of a cardinal, Danny came out in a suit similar to Dons tux. He was all smiles about the responsibility of being a ring bearer. Grace was the flower girl, Danny was ring bearer and Allen as best man Addison's best friend from college was the maid of honor James and Kathleen stood in as secondary for each side. The van with the Bakery advertisement was driving up the gravel road Millie stepped out of the driver seat, already in her formal dress.

She opens the back she unloaded four trays of cookies as well as a five tier cake It was white and laced with a burgundy red. Millie's only hesitation was to greet Laura as she walked by her. with one of the cookie trays. After this she said nothing until he job was done.

Jack sat in the front with Laura leaving the left side open for Quinn. On the other side Doris, George and David had taken front role. As for the rest of the chairs it would seem that the entire town of Shadeland had filled them all.

Don, Allen and Danny's chairs had not been filed yet. Don had taken the opportunity to stroll through the roles of chairs to greet his guest. Some of the guest like Jack, he made personal contact with, and others, like the owner of the pizza place he waved and smile. He made his way up front he stopped to take it in. He paused and turned his head and sat again almost right away. He then stared at his watch and time went on. Allen did the same thing and after being queued by the photographer James did as well. They posing for several more shots from the camera. Don then heard the sound of the car pull up at the end of the role. He poked his neck up trying to see down the aisle. The minister soon motioned to Don. Don stood up and Allen and James did as well. Then the wedding march began. Grace was first to make her way down the aisle. Don could tell that she was excited and she had been using much of her energy not to run down the aisle. She apparently ran out of flowers before she got to the end and had to go back for more so came up the isle again. Kathleen was next her dress it was Burgundy with white lace. Kathleen walked up the aisle with Grace. She adjusted her speed down the aisle so that Addison would be able come in on cue.

The thing that Don realized was that the time it takes a bride to get from the back chair to the front chair had to be the longest ninety second in any man's life. There was also the pause after the minister has asked, if is there anyone that saw just cause why these two should not be joined speak now or ever hold you piece. Don was sure that those words were put in the script just to torment the groom. When Don first saw Addison he wondered how white, a color that contained no color at all could be filled with so much beauty. His first glance of her wedding gown he was blinded with the light seemed to engulf her. When she got close he could see that the light seemed to be coming from her eyes. There were red highlights in her hair that seemed to make her dress sparkle even more and. As she walked hand in hand with Quinn Addison noticed that he was unsteady. Addison squeezed slightly the palm of his hand. He looked at her and began to cry. It seems that it was his turn to watch all the years of their daughter's childhood pass him by. Addison pulled her hand away and locked arms with him in return. He put his palm in top of hers and then looked at her and they both smile. As they reach the front Quinn stops to give her a kiss and takes his seat. The tears flowing freely enough to make him sniffle out loud. The minister asked Who gave this woman to be married. Quinn started to reply but ended up. Breaking down instead. The minister pointed at Quinn and Laura and said that apparently, they do.

The audience had taken their seats and Don and Addison step up to the altar. They look at each other smile and then look at the minister. Don and Addison repeated their vows to each other and there was not one person without a tear. Don had to repeat his twice because the he had been sniffing away in the middle of as I take you hand in mine.

"I Don am aware of and do accept the responsibility of manhood as I take you Addison as my wife"

Don and Addison both gave and received the rings and the minister stated that it was seal and a token of the covenant that they had made. Don, Addison and the minister stood in silence for a moment. Gradually Don and Addison both begin to smile. The minister whispered one more thing in their ear and then turns to the audience and said

"I present to you Don and Addison Lane."

There is completely silent for about five seconds. Then all at once everyone is on their feet, clapping their hands and cheering for the bride and groom. They stood there for what seemed like five minute before they were able to sit down. When they did it was the first time Addison had seen the cake. Not only was it a three tier cake but the cake was made in such way that there was a staircase to the top of it where the bride and groom were. Millie had also made miniature pieces having the appearance of a path way leading to the stairs.

As requested the gifts they received stayed away for household items, they just did not see the need to fill their house with a bunch of things they already had to start with anyway so instead they received gift cards to various restaurants, grocery stores and even one from Home Depot as well. There was a lot of cash as well.

For their honeymoon they would fly to the buffalo springs resort, the place in Lubbock that Don use to fly tourist to. They would spend a week there and just relax. On the way home they were going to stop by Don's house finish cleaning it up and get it ready to sell. They would stop in Dallas to see Dons parents who were not able to be at the wedding. They would then go to an Alabama concert and Finally the last stop before heading home, they had tickets in Fort Worth Texas to see Elton John perform.

Allen stood up took his glass in hand and tapped it in an effort to get the attention of the crowd. He tapped on his glass again and people start to settle down

"Excuse me excuse me hey everyone, I'd like to make a toast to the bride and groom."

He peaked around Don to look at Addison's face. He then told her that he was sure that Don had got the better end of the of this whole thing but he was happy she finally signed the deal. He then said she was the best thing to ever happen to his brother. He lifted his glass and turned to Don to continue his speech. He told Don that the only thing that could have made the day better was if their mom and dad had been there. He then said he thought Don had a great thing going there with Addison and Grace. He also said that honestly in the time that he had been there with them in Indiana he has seen so much of a change and he truly believed it because of those two. Allen said he was grateful for the connections he has made with his kids but also the connection you have helped them make with others. Congratulations Don, congratulation Addison and. He stops to make eye contact with Grace and then back to Don and Addison. Then he said together they made a great team. Then he sat down. Quinn stood up and started to tell them how much he had loved getting to know Don and then Grace. He congratulated Addison for the woman she had become and told several stories about when she was young. He then encouraged them both to make the best of the life they had together.

Don and Addison started to leave tradition told them that they should have run from the wedding party but they ended up just leisurely walking away, Addison had wanted an outside wedding and it had been a boiling hot day and they had used metal chairs for the audience seating. The reason they saw no need to run was instead of throwing rice they blew bubbles at them. This of course was graces favorite part of the day. Allen had put some soap in a small swimming pool and was in the process of extracting a giant bubble using a hula hoop.

Dons plane was their getaway vehicle and Allen had gone all out. He had washed, waxed and shoe polished the side. He put streamers and a basket in the cab with wine cheese spray cheese and crackers

The streamers on the end of the plane were at least a mile and a half long. There was also a net full of helium balloons tied to the end in a way that when they took off they balloons would be released in the air. When Don and Addison climbed in the airplane to leave all the guest had lined each side of the runway and were each holding a balloon

Doris, Allen and Grace stood off to the side as Don started the engine of the plane the crowd started to cheer as it picked up speed and the balloons were released and for a moment or two the plane and the balloons flew side by side. As they departed Allen turned to Doris. He asked her how long it would take Don to realize that to steamers were connected to the barn.

EPILOGUE

Grace ran out the front door and landed on the porch. When she heard the familiar sound of her Grandpa's car she could barely hold herself back, long enough for Quinn to stop. As she did the rest of the family soon appeared. Laura had done it again the back seat and the trunk were full of Laura's casserole dishes and crock pots.

When Laura saw Grace run out she held her arms out wide, bent down and gave her a kiss on the cheek. Then she handed her the bread basket loaded with French bread fresh baked the day before. Behind Grace was James, Kathleen, Don, Allen, Addison and Danny all waiting in line to see what they could carry inside. Quinn watching as the small arm known as his family emptied the car, back seat and trunk included in one foul swoop. They left only the empty turkey roaster by its lonesome in the car. Inside the table had already been set with place settings for all of them as well as enough potholder to hold everything Laura had prepared.

It was not long before the gathering was in full swing. Laura had made chicken fried steak, mash potatoes, gravy, French bread, peas, cranberry bread and brownies and they were all being consumed at a rate faster than anyone had cared to keep track of. At first the only sound that could be heard was the sound of forks on the hitting the plates. Everyone knew that grandmas cooking was going to be good but there was always this moment when they first tasted it that they wanted to do nothing else but enjoy what was there. The chatter did finally begin. Don sat at his place eating cranberry bread and watching interactions between Addison, Grace and the rest of the crowd. Allen is in the seat next to him followed his gaze. A few minutes later Allen spoke up. He asked Don if he still wanted to go home and keep the family farm going, or was he ok with what he had going here.

Don again started reflecting on the years gone by. At one point he wanted to pinch himself to be assured that the image in front of him was actually there and not just a dream.

He was brought back to reality when his eight-year-old daughter climbed in his lap. As they sat together he was struck with the fact that out of all the things he could have asked for out of life this surpassed all his wildest dreams. He had wife and a daughter that mean the world to him, an extended family that brought more joy to him than he could ever imagine. He also had a peace from knowing that whatever troubles life brought his way that he would never have to go through anything alone.

ABOUT THE AUTHOR

Chad Linden grew up in the suburbs of Dallas Texas. No matter what he went through he found his family was always there for him. On the weekends he always spent time with Grandma Lane who was for much of his life was only blocks away. His time with her was spent playing cards, as she told stories about Grandpa George, watching television and emptying her cookie jar. He now lives in a small town of northern California with his Wife and Daughter.

His autobiography "The pages of my life" is available in eBook form on the Amazon Kindle Store.

Printed in the United States
By Bookmasters